DECEPTION AT SANDPIPER BAY

A RILEY HARPER MYSTERY

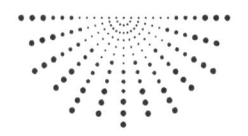

TRACI HALL
PATRICE WILTON

This is a work of fiction. Names, characters, organizations, places, events, and incidents are either products of the author's imagination or are used fictitiously.

Copyright © Traci Hall and Patrice Wilton - October 8, 2023

All rights reserved.

No part of this book may be reproduced, or stored in a retrieval system, or transmitted in any form or by any means, electronic, mechanical, photocopying, or recording, or otherwise, without express written permission of the publisher.

Cover design by Mae from Baby Fresh Designs

Formatted by Bent Elbow Press

BOOK DESCRIPTION

DECEPTION AT SANDPIPER BAY
A RILEY HARPER MYSTERY

DECEPTION IN SANDPIPER BAY, the third book in the award-winning Riley Harper Series, is a thrilling page turner that will keep you reading far into the night and keep you guessing until the startling ending.

During a Fourth of July celebration on Sandpiper Bay—a small island off the coast of Maine—six-year-old Dante Catalina goes missing. The locals are close-knit and friendly but the sea of new faces—strangers boating in, or arriving by ferry to see the fireworks, hinders the investigation. Riley calls in the FBI. She must separate the tangled threads of deceit to find the truth. Her daughter's guilt adds salt to the wound as she realizes Maria, a woman Riley considers a friend, has been lying—for over twenty years.

Every minute is crucial. Every hour Dante is missing potentially puts him farther away from the island.

No contact. No ransom note. Who has Dante? And is that young boy still alive? With the help of her partner, Matt, the chief, and a team of FBI heroes, the countdown to find Dante begins.

PRAISE FOR OUR SALEM B&B COZY MYSTERY SERIES

PRAISE FOR OUR "SALEM B&B COZY MYSTERY SERIES"

Mrs. Morris and the Ghost
Once I started reading, I couldn't put it down. I'm psyched that I discovered this book just in time for the next one. Highly entertaining, incredibly fun read!
"This mystery has everything. Fun, love heartache and suspense! I enjoyed reading and trying to help solve the mystery right along with Mrs. Morris! Can't wait to read another ghost story in this series!"
"I loved this book from the very first page. It was entertaining, the characters were enjoyable, there were surprises along the way, and it is written so well."
"Compelling characters to a well plotted mystery create an engaging read."

Mrs. Morris and the Witch
"The mystery was well- crafted, with plenty of suspense and red herrings to keep me guessing. I highly recommend this one."
"I loved this book. I mean, absolutely loved this book. The Salem B & B Mystery series is fast tracking it's way to my favorite cozy series of all time. It was a fabulous read and I can't wait to see what happens next!"
"How absolutely entertaining! Charlene Morris owns a B&B in Salem and has her own resident ghost. These books are exceptionally well written with fabulous characters. Upon reading these books I feel like I am in Salem visiting all the sights described within. I hope there are many, many more books to come in this series. Highly recommended!!"

Mrs. Morris and the Ghost of Christmas Past

"This is one of the most entertaining series I've read! Extremely well written with great characterization. If you want to leave "real life" behind pick up this book and laugh or gasp or cry or just enjoy the read. Enjoy!"

"This series is just plain awesome!! I love the characters! I love the setting! The B&B is a place I would love to visit and stay at. Just love it all!"

"The Salem B&B Mysteries is quickly becoming one of my favorite cozy mystery series. I enjoyed this third book immensely. The characters are engaging, the setting charming, and I was unable to solve the mystery, which is always a plus. The writing style flows effortlessly, and the wintry Christmas atmosphere will leave you longing for the holiday season."

PRAISE FOR DEATH IN SANDPIPER BAY -- A RILEY HARPER MYSTERY.

Great Series Starter

I absolutely loved this book. Riley Harper is such a great character in this book. I love the feel of the town she moves to. She proves that even though she is a woman officer, she is not one to mess with. Can't wait to see what is in store for Riley next.

After risking everything doing the right thing, Riley Harper packs up her Mum and her daughter and sets off to start over on an island off the coast of Maine. No good deed goes unpunished, and her pasts threatens to destroy her, despite the thousands of miles between then and now. There's a fine line between justice and loyalty...

Having accepted the only precinct willing to take her, Riley is now the newest addition to the Sandpiper Bay Police Department. Riley will have to prove herself worthy or spend the next year in misery. Chief Barnes has let it be known that her being there wasn't at his recommendation...

For the most part, Sandpiper Bay is a community with a low crime rate, so the discovery of a dead girl, who was previously a "local," comes as a shock. Even more shocking, Lacey's death doesn't seem to be mourned by anyone on the island, except for the possibility of her best friend Chloe.

Initially, Chief Barnes seems certain that Lacey's death is suicide, but Riley feels differently. And, when the medical examiner agrees that the death is foul play, the chief designates Riley as lead investigator. With her past working against her, and everyone in town certain that "one of their own" couldn't possibly be the murders, Riley's investigation already has two strikes against it...

Who killed Lacey Killian? Was it an islander or an outsider? Can Riley figure it out, or did all the evidence and her future as an officer get washed out to sea?

Traci Hall & Patrice Wilton have given their readers a fantastic work of mystery/suspense/who dunnit. I look forward to more titles featuring Riley Harper and the rest of the Sandpiper Bay.

Traci Hall and Patrice Wilton are so grateful to our family and book friends who have encouraged us and been so loyal, and enthusiastic! We love you guys who got this ball rolling, asking for more and more books. Traci is bending over backwards to meet your demands.

Patrice is stepping away from the writing process, but she is so delighted and proud of all you wonderful readers that have enjoyed my books, and Traci's of course!

She is my best friend and has unselfishly helped me in so many ways. I've been so lucky to have written ten books with her, but now I can't possibly keep up!

While I'm on the tennis court or traveling and having a different kind of fun, Traci will continue bringing you the wonderful books we all enjoy!

Carry on, Traci, and reach the highest star and accolades that you deserve!

CHAPTER ONE

Saturday morning, Officer Riley Harper stood at the open door of their rented house, allowing the sea breeze and salty air to filter in. Sipping on her Jamaican Island Blue coffee—this week's grocery store special—she thought back to almost eleven months ago when she and her mother Susan, and her daughter Kyra, had moved to Sandpiper Bay, a small island off the coast of Maine. Stepping into this spacious waterfront home, leased for the duration of the contract, had been sunshine to their souls after the emotional beating they'd experienced in Phoenix.

Their world had come crashing down after Riley had testified against her partner in a wrongful death case when he'd shot and killed an unarmed man. She'd been shunned by her fellow police officers as well as friends, who'd also turned their backs on Kyra, forcing them to leave Phoenix under a cloud of shame.

Her current contract expired in six weeks and a decision had to be made—to leave the island for greener pastures or accept Chief Barnes's offer of a permanent position. They'd somehow survived the first months of stress and teenage temper tantrums until the warmth and acceptance from the islanders had slowly wrapped around their hearts.

"What are you doing, Mom?" Her sweet Kyra asked Alexa to play her favorite ear-breaking noise before slinging her slender, gangly arm around Riley's neck and planting a kiss on her cheek.

"I *was* enjoying the morning breeze and listening to the pleasant sounds of nature." Riley smiled at her fifteen-year-old who now stood two inches taller than her, and like a young giraffe, all legs. Her jammies were patterned with red, white, and blue stars. "Are you looking forward to today's festivities? Should be fun."

The island's small population tripled during the summer and quadrupled on holidays like Independence Day—boats dotted the bay from pleasure cruisers to speedboats, almost all sporting the American flag. The Sandpiper Bay Police Department had an arrangement with the Coast Guard for extra manpower to keep folks safe on the water this weekend.

"Yup. Wish you could come with us." Kyra walked over to the fridge and selected a putrid green concoction with extra vitamins and protein, dumped it into the blender on the counter, then pushed the button and whizzed up her breakfast.

Riley's stomach revolted at the look of it, but she kept her mouth shut. Healthy food was great for her daughter but as a cop she lived on donuts, pizza slices, day-old sandwiches, and leftovers. She tried to keep the stale coffee at work to a minimum by bringing her own brew in a stainless-steel mug.

"I'll be there around three-thirty." Stepping into the kitchen next to Kyra, Riley refreshed her coffee and noted the time on her phone. Half past seven and she needed to be at work by eight. She and her partner, Matthew Sniders, were to split the day at the department. She'd asked for the early shift so she could enjoy the Fourth of July festivities at Mackabee Park this afternoon with her mom and Kyra, followed by their favorite lobster dinner... who knew when they'd be able to have fresh lobster again at their whim.

An opulent fireworks display, provided by the Sandpiper Bay fire department, was scheduled for ten that night. Matt would be on duty from two to midnight, with Riley on call if he needed backup. Chief Barnes had one foot out the door thanks to some health issues and was in Portland with his wife and grandbabies.

"I need to change and get out of here before I get fired," Riley said as a joke. They both knew that threat was long gone. Now the chief was nearly begging her to stay.

"Fired," her mother laughed. In her slippers, Susan's steps down the staircase had been silent as a whisper. She gave her granddaughter a kiss, saving one for Riley. "That would be too easy. You can't keep dragging your feet. We've got to let the leasing agent know if we want this house for another year."

Riley sipped her coffee and hid a grimace from her mom. "I know." She turned to her daughter as Kyra finished the mossy-green sludge. "I promised I would have my answer to the chief by July fifteenth—if we don't stay, he'll have to hire someone else."

Until April, her teenager had been eager to move to a bigger town or back to Phoenix, but then she'd made a wonderful friend who was also a budding artist, Lennie Banks. The girls had become inseparable. Lennie had convinced her art teacher to invite Kyra to Paris for a ten-day immersive arts course as someone had backed out. It was leaving next week.

Kyra had waffled from moving off the island to staying with her new best friend. Sammie in Phoenix had been her best bud, but they'd grown apart. She wiped her mouth with her forearm and rinsed the blender rather than comment. Her daughter had become evasive regarding a simple yes or no answer. And was it fair for Riley to expect one?

Susan squeezed Riley's shoulder in silent commiseration and

took the mug. Her mother would travel to the ends of the earth with them no matter where they ended up. "Do you have time for an egg sandwich?"

"I could take one with me. Thanks, Mom." Riley hurried up the stairs.

When they'd first arrived, Kyra was apprehensive about the three of them sharing the same roof, but her mother was a godsend, managing the house and keeping peace when tensions ran high.

Solving two murders in less than a year, plus dealing with blizzards and hurricanes could drive anyone batty, but all three women had held strong.

Bradley Barnes had made her life hell when she'd first arrived, but her skills at solving crimes with Matthew had gained the chief's respect. He'd started having medical problems and his wife wanted him to retire. Though Matthew had grown up on the island and knew every nook and cranny, Riley had more experience in the police force, so he'd asked her to take over his position.

The decision was not easy for Riley to make. Kyra had been miserable for so long before befriending Lennie. As a mother, she understood that being a teenager on a remote island had disadvantages. Kyra rode the ferry to and from Bangor each day where she attended high school and connected with other teens in the arts. During the summer, she didn't have that stimulation.

The tightknit community in Sandpiper Bay had welcomed her and her family with open arms but Riley feared they deserved better opportunities than what was offered. With that in mind, she'd put together her resume and sent out feelers for the job market.

Matt, her partner in crime, deserved an answer too. She enjoyed his company, his great sense of humor, and his logical sensibility when it came to law enforcement. Small island. Big hearts. Hard to give up.

Ugh! Riley pulled on her blue knee-length summer uniform, tucked in her short-sleeved shirt, and placed her revolver safely into her holster. She trotted down the steps, grabbed her to-go breakfast, and gave her mom and Kyra hugs. "I'm off at three-thirty. I'll call and see where you guys are so we can meet up."

She climbed into her SUV and started the engine, driving toward the station. The picturesque island surrounded by clear blue water was heavily wooded, with lots of one-way dirt roads. Two teenaged girls around Kyra's age stepped from the bushes as Riley rounded a corner.

Riley's wheels spun as she slammed on her brakes and lay on the horn. She was rewarded by the finger from both young ladies. Scantily dressed in bikini tops and short-shorts, with multi-colored hair, they wore smug smiles on their pretty faces.

By staying here another year could she delay the process of Kyra growing into a bad-ass know-it-all teenager? The change had already begun but Susan was a smart woman and ruled her grandchild with a firm but loving hand.

Riley parked the SUV in front of the Sandpiper Bay Police Station and hopped out. She mopped her brow and glanced up at the clear blue sky. Just a few minutes after eight and it was already in the low eighties; by mid-afternoon it would be hotter than Hades.

She had her keys out to unlock the door and was startled when it swung open. Matthew stood there grinning and waved a steaming cup of coffee under her nose. "Deli Donuts at your service."

Riley laughed. "Perfect. Mom made an egg sandwich which I will happily share."

Due to the holiday only Matt and herself were manning the station. Nancy worked at the front desk Monday through Friday and Rosita, a civilian officer, worked full-time, but her schedule varied depending on her community outreach commitments.

Light jazz played over the speakers as Riley followed the cheerful redhead to the staff's kitchen at the rear of the building. What had put him in such a good mood? Why was he here when he wasn't supposed to show up until two or three?

Though not yet thirty, Matthew had been born and raised in Sandpiper Bay and had earned his stripes. Was he hoping to make Chief and have the seat she might refuse?

Holding her bag and keys in one hand and the hot coffee in the other, Riley used her foot to kick out a chair. She fell into it and cradled the stainless-steel mug as Matt whistled to the sweet sound of the horns.

"Nice music," Riley said. Matt handed her two paper plates from the side counter and a knife, so she divided the sandwich in half then placed them on the plates with the six pack of donuts between them.

He was grinning ear to ear, like a kid on his birthday.

"Come on, Matt, cough it up. You should still be in bed, or kayaking, or maybe fishing? Something. The weather's perfect and not too hot yet."

He lowered his voice, as if anyone was there to listen. "I met someone last week when I went to Bangor for a dental appointment."

Matt blushed so hard that she almost felt sorry for him. "Was she the dentist or dental hygienist?" Not that it mattered.

"Dentist intern. Dr. Collins hired Laura as an assistant for the summer. It's her final year before she graduates and has her degree." His ruddy cheeks bloomed in embarrassment. "She's so smart. I don't know why she wanted to come here this weekend, but she asked if we could meet up."

"Because she is smart and knows a good thing when she sees it." Riley couldn't be happier for Matt, who hadn't really been involved since his fiancé had dumped him for the big city.

"So now I'm a thing, am I?" Matthew brushed a lock of hair from his face, swallowing the half sandwich in two bites. "I'm waiting for the ferry. Laura and her friend are going to be on the nine o'clock." He passed Riley his phone, showing her a picture of a pretty brunette with a beautiful smile. "She just turned thirty."

"That's great. Have a good time and remember that you're pretty darn special yourself." Riley would miss their easy banter if she left the island. "Tell her about the murders you solved, that should impress her."

"You think so?" His brows rose in alarm.

"Not if you want to see her again." Riley snickered.

"Smart ass." He stood and shook off crumbs from his lap then nudged the remaining donuts her way. "I should be back around two-thirty or so. If I'm not here, you can probably figure out where I might be." Again, his face flamed.

"Matt—where would that be?" Riley teased and hoped that Laura was worth Matt's shyness. He was a gentleman to the core.

"Can't say for sure." Nerves made his voice shake. He must really like this woman. "I'll play it by ear and keep the ringer on."

"You better! I don't mind if you're a little late, but I promised Kyra I'd meet them at the park around three-thirty."

Matthew pocketed his phone. "No worries."

"Have fun. You deserve it." As he sauntered by, Riley grabbed his wrist. There was one sure thing that would be a buzzkill for a fledgling romance. "Just don't find any dead bodies today, please."

"I'll do my best, but no promises." With a jaunty wave, Matthew left her alone with the donuts. Riley quickly hid them behind the cans of soda in the near-empty refrigerator. Out of sight, out of mind.

With Matt gone, Riley attacked the pile of paperwork on her desk. Though tedious, it needed attention. She'd pushed off an answer long enough.

In her heart she would love to stay another year. Her mom was on board having made friends at the library where she'd organized a book club. Kyra had wanted to move but only changed her mind after meeting Lennie and discovering a natural talent for art.

Riley had to be the adult here and make the hard decisions. The earth was large, and the island small. She didn't want to limit Kyra's view of the world or diminish her opportunity to become all that she could be.

Riley wanted the three of them to come to an informed, mutual decision that would benefit them all but admitted that it might not be possible.

Leafing through her personal drawer, Riley pulled out the resume she'd put together. It included a brief but accurate description of her life's work and how she'd ended up on this remote island. Her pride and fifteen-year career demanded that much. Five places had openings that perked her interest.

One charming city tempted her with its population of less than 30,000—Portsmouth, New Hampshire. Boston, Massachusetts seemed nice. Lots of history there. Smaller than Phoenix but not too small. Chicago, Miami, and Washington D.C. were perfectly good runners-up. She dismissed the most appealing, which was Maui, as it was another island and weren't they trying to avoid just that?

She glanced at the calendar and July 15th circled in red. Nine days to let the chief know. Tick, tock.

Her inbox dinged an incoming message. It was from PHXPD, her old police department in Phoenix. Pulse thudding in her ears, she clicked the tab to open the message. What could they possibly want?

Riley didn't recognize the name, Officer Marcy Kendricks. Apparently there had been a shift of power in the past year and this Marcy person wondered if she'd be willing to overlook the grievous wrongdoings she'd suffered in the department.

Everyone involved had been dismissed and they would like Riley to set up a training department for new recruits. Her salary would be adjusted to as if she'd never left. Full benefits. It was a shame what had happened to her for telling the truth. Marcy, on behalf of Phoenix PD, was very sorry.

Her heart pounded in her chest and a wave of nausea rose in her stomach. She knew she wouldn't go back. That episode was a shut case. Even the idea of being in Phoenix made her physically ill.

Bad memories surfaced like stab wounds to the gut. The unfairness of it all still held a bitter taste, but when it had filtered down as low as tormenting her daughter, there'd never be forgiveness.

She didn't answer the email. No way in hell. It had taken this island and being with officers and people who had integrity to return her faith in law enforcement.

Her phone rang and she pushed back from her desk. Kyra's face shone from the screen. Probably wanted to know if Riley could get off even earlier. "What's up, honey? Having fun?"

Her daughter burst into sobs. "Mom, you've got to get here fast. Dante is missing and it's all my fault."

Dante was Maria Catalina's six-year-old son. Kyra occasionally babysat him, and she adored the little boy. Maria owned Piazza Pizza and had become close friends with Riley and her family. Maria cherished her sweet son.

Riley remembered when Kyra had been around four and she'd slipped free of her hand in a department store. It had been the worst five minutes of Riley's motherhood, not knowing where her daughter had gone. Kyra had been hiding under some clothes thinking she was playing a game, but she never forgot that helpless fear in the pit of her belly. "Calm down, sweetheart. When was the last time that you saw him? He's probably nearby."

"I don't know exactly! We were playing with the bubble machine." Kyra sniffled. "He loves bubbles."

Riley hated the distraught tone in her daughter's voice. "Let me talk to Nana, honey. It's okay. He might be playing with some neighbor kids and just wandered off. We will find him."

"Just come!" Kyra wailed, then she gave the phone to Susan.

"Hello, Riley." Her mother sounded concerned. This made Riley concerned, because her mother was the calmest woman she'd ever known.

"Mom. When was the last time that you saw Dante, for sure?"

"We were eating hot dogs, so lunch time. Kyra had promised him an ice cream if he ate it all, but then he saw the bubble machine and thought that was more fun. He wanted to get ice cream later."

Riley read the time on her phone. One-fifteen. She swallowed hard. "When did you guys arrive?"

"Ten, to help Maria set up her Piazza Pizza booth. We'd offered to keep an eye on Dante while she and her employees got ready for the lunch crowd, then she was going to join us on the blanket to watch the acrobats on stage at one."

Riley jotted down those details on a piece of notepaper on her desk. "Does she know that you can't find Dante?"

"Yes, we told her. Kyra feels awful, but honestly, the park is very crowded. Dante would recognize the pizza booth and go there, don't you think, if he got lost?"

"I'm on my way." In all the excitement, the little boy might have been chasing a bubble without a thought to staying with Kyra. He'd grown up on the island and didn't know a "stranger." Riley ended the call and closed her computer, patting the gun at her hip. She picked up her small bag and locked the door behind her.

On route to Mackabee Park, Riley called Matt, who didn't pick up. She hoped he was having lunch with Laura and hated to interrupt. She left a quick message. The place was packed, with children running around, kites flying behind them. Food booths, laughter. Picnic blankets on the green lawn and camp chairs facing the bandstand. She parked the Hyundai on the edge of the grass for quick access. If Dante was still missing, these folks would need to be interviewed. A search party formed. But she was getting ahead of herself.

The woods were to the right side, between the park and the ocean. The ferry would be to the east, the fishing docks to the west. The southern part of the island was populated with nicer homes. In the center of the park, a metal stage had been erected. Different acts would perform during the day, and rock music at night. This meant the island was heavy with tourists and performers. *Strangers.*

Riley scanned the packed lawn for any sign of Dante's dark brown curls but didn't see them. She followed the scent of tomato and garlic. Kyra waved when she spotted her weaving through the holiday crowd, then threw herself into Riley's arms, sobbing. Riley held her daughter tight murmuring consoling words. Susan put her arms around them both in a family hug. Riley pulled back and looked at Maria, standing a few feet away with fear in her eyes.

"Riley!" Maria said, her voice catching. She wore a patriotic sundress of red, white, and blue with a half apron around her waist. "I've looked all over. Dante's not here."

Coby, her boyfriend, comforted her. "I'm sure he wandered off and got lost. He'll be found soon."

Riley could only hope he was right.

CHAPTER TWO

Riley strode to the fretful mother and gently touched Maria's shoulder. She had to put aside their friendship to interview her. "Maria...hey."

Maria wiped her flushed cheeks and grabbed Riley's arm. "Help me find Dante. He's got to be around here somewhere, I know it."

Time was of the essence. Riley had learned as an officer in Phoenix that every 40 seconds a child goes missing or is abducted in the United States. She had seen her share of cases; some had gone bad, while in others the child had been found quickly and returned home to their families. "When exactly did you last see him?"

Maria glanced at Coby. "I'm not sure. Can you remember?"

"Had to be when he was having lunch." Coby looked around frantically. "Must have been around noon, maybe a little later?"

"Maria, in cases like this when a child goes missing, they are usually found within six hours," Riley said. "So, we need to act fast. Please try to remember everything you can."

"He was eating a hot dog on this blanket with Kyra." Maria tapped her toe to an old king-sized bed cover. Susan and Kyra had large beach towels and camp chairs to the side. "I was at the pizza booth with Jessica." Her chin quivered. "Dante was excited about the acrobats and waved at me with a huge grin."

"What can we do to help?" Coby stayed with Maria, but it was clear to read the frustration on his tanned face.

Riley gestured around them. "Where have you looked?"

"All over the park." Maria's voice trembled. "What if he's in the woods? We need more searchers. Dogs. Can we get bloodhounds?"

It was difficult to forecast this situation. The probability was great that Dante was nearby but on the off chance that he'd been taken, Riley had to follow protocol. "We would get them from the police department in Bangor, which would take time. We can't wait." Where was Matthew? She pulled out her phone and texted him.

Dante's missing. Get to Mackabee's fast.

Riley peered at the pizza booth where a line of ten people waited for food. Jessica, blonde, maybe twenty, templed her hands in a prayer as she caught Riley's eye, then resumed serving the line of customers. They'd met at Piazza Pizza when Maria had hired the girl for the summer position. Lots of places on the coast offered seasonal employment.

Parker, a tall, thin, twenty-three-year-old with shoulder-length hair normally worn in a bun, was the other employee and full-time year-round.

Coby stepped closer to Maria, offering support. "He'll come wandering back any second now." He hugged her briefly, a worried expression on his handsome face. The false cheer was intended to comfort Maria but had the opposite effect. Maria dropped to her knees with a moan of despair.

Riley felt sick to her stomach. Statistics, and memories of her career in Phoenix, floated to the surface as Maria broke apart. Dante needed to be found. Soon.

She'd contemplated working for Child Crime Prevention,

but the statistics were too overwhelming and sad. At that time, she'd been married to an abuser and Kyra was only two.

The numbers were staggering. Approximately 840,000 children were reported missing each year, and family abductions led the list by half, with bitter divorces and custody battles. Female perpetrators outnumbered the male. It was a nightmare for law officials.

Acquaintances and strangers made up the second largest abductions and typically occurred in outdoor locations. Riley couldn't share that information right now.

"We'll give Dante another ten minutes, and if he doesn't show up, we'll get a search party going." The kidnapping cases Riley had been involved with before had left a scar as she'd always imagined Kyra as the one taken. "Maria, is there any chance he would have gone home?"

"On his own? No! That's two miles away and he's only six." Maria drew in a shaky breath. "I bet he wandered off and got lost. He must be so scared right now." A tear spilled down her cheek.

Rosita, the community liaison at the station, joined Riley and Maria. She was in civilian clothes as this was her day off. "Hi! Is everything okay? You all look worried."

"Dante is missing," Riley said calmly. "Will you help me set up a search party grid for the park?"

"Sure." Rosita's gaze narrowed. "No problem, but do you think it's come to that?"

"Better safe than sorry, my friend." Riley locked eyes with Coby. "Want to help Rosita?"

Coby's jaw tightened with concern. "Yeah. Tell me what to do. I've already walked this whole area."

"A grid is different," Riley explained. "And it doesn't help that Dante is six and probably not sitting in one place, right?"

Maria brushed her auburn hair off her forehead. The breeze

from the ocean was the only thing keeping them all from melting. "Dante never sits still."

"He likes to run," Kyra said.

Maria shifted to ignore Kyra, her face stern.

Riley hurt for her daughter at the snub but kept her patience. "Maria, you can be home base on the blanket. Everyone, make sure that your ringers are on so we can stay in touch via text. Most likely Dante will be back before I finish making the announcement."

Maria studied her phone and then dropped it in her apron pocket. "God, I hope so. He has to."

Riley put a hand on her shoulder knowing that Maria needed to remain strong and positive. Kyra and Susan stayed on the blanket too, wanting to help, their powerless expressions clear to read.

Riley turned to Rosita and Coby. "Let's go. I'll make an announcement from the stage. Rosita and Coby, you'll be search party leaders. We'll make a grid and cover every inch of this park, then, if necessary, tackle the woods." She lowered her voice, "Time is of the essence. While you are combing the park and surrounding area, I'll take Maria home."

"Why?" Coby glanced over his shoulder toward Maria, watching from the blanket. "Hey—would a kidnapper want a ransom?"

"We'll need to see if Dante is there," Riley said. "And gather information."

Rosita already had a map of the park open on her phone and sent it by airdrop to Coby. "In this type of situation, it's recommended that we separate the area into grids and search with small groups of four to five people."

"Yep. That sounds about right," Riley said. "Let's see how many volunteers we can drum up."

Riley hurried to the stage and climbed the steps, Rosita and Coby on her heels. A man was playing guitar but stopped when she asked for the microphone. He got up and out of the spotlight.

"Good afternoon, Sandpiper Bay!" Riley waited until she had most of the Fourth of July reveler's eyes on her. Folks elbowed one another.

"We would love your help here today. A resident of our island, Dante Catalina, is missing. Probably wandered off after some bubbles, but we need your help to locate him. He's six years old, with brown eyes and brown curly hair. If you find him, take him to the Piazza Pizza booth to the right of the stage. To keep this system in order, please join my assistants here, Rosita, and Coby, to make sure we don't miss an inch. Thank you!"

Questions erupted, but Riley didn't have answers. She raised her palm in a signal for quiet. "If you'd like to help, come to the stage and we will assign you an area."

Riley used the advantage of being on the stage to peer around the crowd, but the familiar brown curls weren't in sight. Her stomach clenched and she had a bad feeling. Where could he be?

Darren Williams was the first to volunteer for the search. An army vet suffering from PTSD, Darren lived in the lighthouse and had been a recluse for years. He would know the territory very well. Coby and Darren, heads bowed, whispered together. Their expressions conveyed determination to find the little boy.

After that, a flood of islanders joined Rosita and Coby to help. Rosita had them organized into ten parties of five. Riley wished she could join them, but her part of the plan was to check Maria's house. As she left the stage, she saw that Kyra and Susan remained with Maria, who was on the phone. Had Dante been located?

Matt Snider pushed his way through the ragged line of concerned islanders. Their backs formed a partial barricade but quickly cleared when they realized who it was. Their own

DECEPTION AT SANDPIPER BAY

Matthew Sniders, officer of the law. Not in uniform but clearly a leader. Unfortunately, along with recognition came a great many questions. He waved them off and marched ahead.

Riley touched his shoulder. "Glad you're here, Matt—we could really use your expertise. You must know all the trails in this park. I'm sorry I had to pull you away."

Matt raised his hand. "What's going on?" He quickly took in Maria's tears, Kyra, Coby, and Rosita. People holding phones with the map of the park to begin the quest. The murmurs of the islanders. "You sent a text that Dante was missing?"

"Yes, that's right."

Matthew winced. "How long?"

"Since lunchtime. Probably between noon and twelve thirty." It would need to be narrowed down if Dante remained...gone. "He had his lunch then decided to play with the bubble machine. That was when Kyra and my mom lost sight of him."

"Oh, no," Matt said, understanding right away that Kyra probably felt responsible. "Kids are notorious for dashing off to the next adventure. Want me to join one of the rescue parties, or help you sort things out here?"

"Could you oversee the search party? Rosita is amazing but she's being mobbed by the volunteers. I'm taking Maria home, to check if Dante is there." Riley prayed he was because the alternative sucked. "Or, in case there's a call." Sometimes a kidnapping resulted in a request for ransom though not often. Usually, it was a clear desire for custody, or for ill intent.

"You got it." Matt was more than ready to jump into action. "Stay in touch. I will too. Hopefully this will end in a celebration, and Dante simply wandered off."

"My thoughts exactly." Riley agreed fervently. "Where's Laura?"

"She and her friend are checking in at their VRBO."

"Once we find Dante, she'll think you're a hero."

17

Matt chuckled even as he blushed. "I doubt that. So, have you interviewed anyone? Someone must have seen something."

"Not yet. Figured the search party was the most important. Rosita organized it perfectly." Rosita's position meant that she was basically an officer but couldn't arrest anyone and didn't carry a gun, but she'd had criminal investigation training.

"If this first search doesn't find him, we'll call the station in Bangor. A missing kid?" Matthew shrugged. "Volunteers will be no problem."

"Next step, after talking with Barnes, is to contact the FBI." This was where Riley's experience came into play. "Let's get moving. Poor Dante will be frantic."

"How's Maria holding up?" Matthew sent a discreet glimpse her way. Susan tried to console Maria while Kyra paced back and forth.

"Not well," Riley said. "She'll be better once she has Dante back in her arms."

"We all will be, for sure. Kid's as cute as they get." Matthew rubbed the side of his nose. "You've gotten friendly with Maria. Does she ever talk about Dante's dad?"

In the past year, Maria hadn't mentioned Dante's father, and neither had Coby. The man was obviously out of the picture. "Not really."

"I've read that it's often the non-custodial parent in a missing children's case." Smart. Matthew might not have as many years in the field, but he was still a very competent police officer.

"You're right." Riley nodded as Rosita walked their way, the folks she'd gathered behind her at the stage. "I'll question Maria about him if we don't locate Dante."

Rosita caught up with them. "Good to see you, Matt. All filled in?"

"Yup." Matthew read his phone free as a ping sounded.

"Just sent you the map. Follow me," Rosita said in a firm voice.

Rosita led Matt and Riley toward the waiting volunteers. Once on the edge of the crowd, she stopped and faced them. Riley and Matt stood on either side of her in a united front. "We have ten groups of five. All ten leaders should know their grid and stay within the assigned area. If you see anything suspicious or a possible clue, tell your leader."

"What happens then?" a tall, scruffy blond asked. His group of four mulled around him.

"Call me. I'll be supervising the search from the park." Matthew stepped forward. "And keep everyone in the loop so we don't interfere. I'll send my number to the group chat."

Rosita checked her watch. "If anyone has a question now is the time." No one raised a hand. "Let's reconvene here when we've completed the search, which should take no more than an hour."

Matthew inched back next to Riley. Her gaze went to the woods near the park and a shiver ran over Riley's flesh. "Matthew, you lived here years ago when all those stories of children going missing terrorized the island. Could this be…"

"No!" Matt said emphatically. "That was mostly nonsense anyway."

Riley wasn't so sure. Chief Barnes had been convinced when he'd told her to keep Kyra out of the woods a year ago. Islanders still believed it was cursed.

Her skin prickled. The July Fourth celebration skirted the deeper, mysterious woods that had supposedly swallowed up several young children over the years. It had to be a myth, one of those campfire stories told in the dark to scare each other. Had they made all this up, or was there a more sinister truth?

Darren whistled. "My group will take the far side of the park. Let's go." Riley trusted this ex-marine who suffered from PTSD. He'd lived alone in the lighthouse for years, scouring the woods for food with a rifle on his back and a bow and arrow for smaller kills. She once had mistakenly believed he could be a killer but ended up with egg on her face. The war had done a number on him, but he was a simple man who enjoyed his solitude. Not much to ask when he'd given so much.

"Wait for me!" A woman with a sunburned nose and a turquoise-blue Sandpiper Bay T-shirt rushed to Riley and Matthew. "I have experience with tracking. I'm Patricia."

"Welcome!" Riley pointed her to Rosita's group. "You'll be helpful then. Thank you so much."

The search would be methodical; people eager to assist. Riley knew the islanders would turn the park upside down to find Dante and rid the island of the gloom that had settled over the folks who'd come for the festivities.

Riley walked toward the pizza booth to get the lay of the park from that angle. Kyra had her eyes on the open area where Dante had gone missing. Susan stayed to comfort Maria. They sat on the two lawn chairs to see the park better. Her mother had been a neo nurse and was a rock in an emergency.

Alone with her thoughts, Riley went through different scenarios. What if Dante had fallen into one of the creeks that meandered through the forest? The creek bed would be dry this time of the year, so drowning was not an issue. If he injured his leg or been knocked out, he might not have been able to cry for help.

That outcome would be much better than the alternative.

Her trained eye took in everything at once. Food carts, drink stands, simple games to amuse the children. Throwing darts to pop a balloon and win a prize, another stand had a soft hammer to punch little animated squirrels that popped up before they got back into their holes again. The bubble machine created bubbles so big you could jump into them and make them burst. A teenager cranked the wheel, grinning at the laughing kids. It didn't make sense that Dante would just disappear when the fun was here.

Riley's stomach churned, dread replacing any joy that could have been. Every decent cop knew that timing was the key to finding a child. Each minute that passed led him farther away.

This was a small island, she reminded herself. Not a big city where multiple crimes were committed each day. She lifted her head to the sky hoping for clarity. Startled, she rapidly blinked her eyes, and it was still there. A bright colorful balloon floating over the treetops. Had Dante seen one too, and gone to follow?

Close to an hour had passed since her arrival, and no sign of Dante by the search parties. She tried not to worry but the facts were hard to dismiss. Dante could have wandered off but if so, he should have been found by now. She returned to the blanket. This instant, that sweet child might be in the hands of someone who wanted to harm him.

"Where is Dante?" Maria demanded, out of patience.

"He will be found," Riley said, making a vow that she hoped she could keep. She turned to her daughter and saw the fear in Kyra's eyes. She put her hands on her daughter's arms. "Sweetheart, we will search day and night, all right?"

Kyra gave a brave smile that showed she wanted to believe but was scared stiff.

"He'll be home for dinner, just you wait and see." Susan spoke as if to reassure herself as much as Kyra, Riley, and Maria. "Should we look elsewhere?"

"No! We can't leave. It's all my fault," Kyra whispered. "I should have watched him more closely. Instead, I got distracted by a couple of girls who were messing around with some guys from school. They aren't from here, just summer girls."

Riley had to bite her tongue. One year ago, Kyra would've considered the girls cool, but now thought them outsiders. That had to be some kind of progress. Or was it?

It was half past two. Nearly two hours had gone by since

Dante had been seen and not one sighting since. Maria's chin wobbled as she snagged Riley's hand. "I'm not leaving this spot. I won't. It's the last place I saw Dante."

Riley understood Maria's emotions, one mother to another. Just as she wanted to protect Kyra from blaming herself or being chastised for neglect.

"I have a way that all of you can help," Riley said. "Mom, Kyra, you stay here and wait for Dante's return. Keep the prayers going and hold onto your faith."

Kyra scrunched her nose to argue.

Riley raised her palm. "Maria, I know you said Dante wouldn't go home, but it's protocol for us to check and cross that out, all right?"

"I just told you that I don't want to leave!" Maria exclaimed.

"We don't have a choice." Riley relented at the woman's pained expression. "If possible, I'll bring you back."

"What about Wyatt?" Susan asked. Her mother and the ferry captain had become friends over the past few months. "Should we ask him if he's seen Dante? Alert him to what's going on?"

"Yes." Was it any reason that Riley relied on Susan in an emergency? "That would be great, but on the down-low, okay?"

Susan nodded.

"Let's go." Riley took Maria's arm and led her toward the edge of the grass where her vehicle was parked, keeping her voice relaxed. "There are rules to follow for situations like this."

Riley knew the steps she had to take if Dante wasn't at his home: Call Chief Barnes, contact the FBI. Get Dante in the system. Find out if kind Maria had any secrets.

"Where's Matthew?" Maria asked.

"Matthew's overseeing the search. We will leave no stone unturned." Riley met Maria's gaze as they reached the SUV. "Everything will work out. We have an island of people looking for Dante. What better odds?"

Riley opened the passenger door and waited for Maria to get

settled before walking around and jumping into the driver's seat of her wonderful Hyundai. During a crazy storm last December, she'd lost the Fiat—may it rest in peace—and the chief had relented, buying her a second-hand SUV.

"I'm telling you that Dante won't be there," Maria groused all the way from the park to her front door, a five-minute drive. "This is a waste of time."

"Let's just wait and see. Give the volunteers a chance." If the little boy wasn't there, check for clues as to Dante's location.

Before leaving the car, Riley quickly bowed her head and asked for help. Rules were great, but a few prayers never hurt.

CHAPTER THREE

They arrived at the bungalow that Maria had bought twenty years ago. Maria was an artist as well as the owner of Piazza Pizza and had painted her home in bright seaside corals and blues. The yard had a four-foot white picket fence around green grass. The roof was slate and seemed new. A slate chimney was off center to the right of the blue front door.

Riley parked on the street. Maria got out slowly, studying her house as if she could tell just by looking if her son was inside. She opened the gate, and Riley followed the slate path. Vibrant and abundant flowerpots lined the porch.

Maria unlocked the door, then looked back at Riley. "It's still locked. That's good, right?"

"Can I go before you?" Riley patted her hip, the holster with her weapon at her side.

Maria straightened. "It's fine. I know the house is empty."

Riley heightened her senses, her hand flexed as Maria entered. The foyer had been redone with a child in mind. Tile for the floor, boots and shoes lined up below lower hooks with rain jackets, sweatshirts, or sweaters. Taller hooks for the adults to place their things. Umbrellas in a stand.

Maria released a breath, conveying to Riley that they were again wasting time.

Riley had often been a guest at Maria's home and knew the layout. Kitchen was to the left, and bedrooms to the right. The guest bath was off the hall, the master suite had its own. Riley followed Maria to Dante's room. The interior had been painted with circus animals, the walls blue, the comforter and furniture perfect for a little boy. This wasn't a child neglected in any way.

Maria's gaze paused on a partially open bottom drawer. The four-foot-tall chest had two drawers and a lion lamp on top.

"What is it?" Riley asked.

Maria shook her head and pulled her gaze from the drawer.

"Do your best to remember. Any small detail can be important." Riley crossed the room and opened the closet, then looked under the bed. Dante wasn't there.

Maria rubbed her arms and slowly opened the drawer as if afraid it held a snake. She gasped and rummaged through the items. "His new clothes for school are gone." Her voice broke. Quickly, she opened the drawer above it. "His favorite Paw Patrol pajamas are missing too."

Riley tensed, wishing she hadn't let Maria touch the knobs. "Anything else?"

"A few toys, but not his favorite stuffed lion. That makes no sense." Maria whirled around, staring at Riley in a daze. "Dante wouldn't have walked home on his own," she said in a gravelly voice. "And he certainly wouldn't take his clothes with him."

Damn it. "He wasn't alone, Maria. Someone brought him here." Riley's skin dotted with apprehension. *Call Barnes. The FBI.* How did one go about locking down an island?

Maria shook her head vehemently, unwilling to accept the simple truth. Her body quaked and she leaned against the wall. "No! We should be at the park, for when they find him. He'll want me." The curvy auburn-haired beauty was normally an exuberant personality given to quick hugs and deep laughter, not this sorrowful figure in deep denial.

The woman was in shock. Riley led Maria to the kitchen, making a mental note of what they each touched, and poured her a glass of chilled water. Behind the closed door was an attached garage and laundry room. The master suite was on the opposite side of the house. There was a second entrance near the office that opened to a large yard. Eager to search the place top to bottom, Riley couldn't leave Maria now or risk her friend breaking to pieces.

"Any word on your cell?" Riley noted there was no blinking red light to signal a message on the house phone.

Maria had put her mobile down and was staring out the kitchen window, so Riley snuck a quick look for a recent notification, but the screen was blank, other than a picture of Dante as the screen saver.

Maria was in complete denial. Was it possible that this morning she might have innocently activated the situation? An argument, or harsh words could be misconstrued, but Riley believed it would take much more than that for Dante to run away.

Clearing her throat, Riley asked, "Tell me Maria, about how your morning went? Was there anything different or unusual?"

"Of course! It's the Fourth of July," Maria said shortly. "Dante was excited to get to the park and see the acrobats." Her mouth twitched the slightest bit toward a smile. "He wants to join the circus when he grows up, like a character on his favorite cartoon."

"I think I saw an episode or two when he was over, and Kyra was babysitting. A lion runs the circus?"

"Yes." Maria glanced at Riley. "How could Kyra have lost him? I'm trying really hard not to be angry or blame her. I didn't hire her to babysit today, we were all just watching him. Coby, Jessica. Susan. Parker. Like any other day."

Riley's first reaction was to defend Kyra, which would not help Maria right now. "It was an accident. Maria, let's focus on the time you saw him last, as close to exact as you can get."

"I'll do my best." Maria shut her eyes for a moment and rubbed her arms. "He was eating a hot dog and chips," she said. "On the blanket next to Kyra."

After a pause, Riley asked, "What was he wearing?"

Maria answered quickly. "A red, white, and blue striped shirt. Blue shorts, blue sandals with the back strap so they don't fall off when he runs."

"Was he wearing a cap? Sunglasses?"

"No." Maria blinked fast. "I don't know what time it was! How can I not know?"

Maria's phone dinged with a text notification.

"News?" Riley asked hopefully.

"No." Maria's mouth pursed in anger as she studied the message. "My idiot cousins want to talk and now is not the best time, obviously."

"Where do they live? Brooklyn?" Riley knew Maria still had family there but was not on friendly terms. In fact, when Maria had gone back last month for her father's funeral, she'd had Dante stay with Riley for two nights.

"Don't know and don't care as long as they are far away from me." Maria spun a silver band on her pinky.

Riley watched her friend closely. Maria liked her rings, having one on each finger except where a wedding ring might be. What was going on in her head? "Anything else you want to add?"

"Not really. I just want my son back."

Riley's frustration grew. How far could she pry without Maria shutting down completely? And why was she so reluctant to speak about her past? Despite their friendship, Maria continued to keep her past under lock and key.

Maria had a huge heart and was incredibly talented in both the kitchen and as an artist. She was passionate.

Could that mean having a temper? Had Dante behaved badly in some way that had triggered an overreaction of some kind? Hard to believe but as a police officer Riley had to scrutinize every angle.

"I need to look at his bedroom again." Maria dropped her phone into her apron pocket and pushed away from the kitchen counter, moving unsteadily toward Dante's room. "This makes no sense."

"Be careful not to touch anything." Riley followed her slowly as she checked her messages. Not a single word from Matthew or Rosita. She did a cursory scan of the living room, but nothing appeared out of place. She needed to search the whole home.

Riley sat Maria on the edge of Dante's bed and peered into her friend's eyes. Maria smoothed her sundress over her knees, fiddling with the apron. "It's imperative that you tell me all you can. If Dante was abducted, we've got to shut the island down. Is there anybody you can think of who might take him?"

"No." Maria swallowed hard. "Not here anyway."

"Could your family mean you harm? You said they are all in Brooklyn and the Bronx, is that right?"

"Probably. I have no connection with them," Maria said. "My uncle was a controlling jerk. He bullied my dad." She tugged her phone from the apron pocket. "My crazy cousins are just like him." Her jaw clenched as she read the notifications.

Riley wished she could see Maria's screen. "You learned the restaurant business from your dad, didn't you?"

Maria crossed her arms, eyes welling as she examined the ceiling.

"Basically. I grew up at the family pizzeria. My parents are dead," Maria said at last. "Mom and Dad both. I don't know that

I ever told you about my mom?" Her cheeks flushed with emotion.

Riley shook her head, backing away from Maria to give the woman room to breathe. "Did you get along?"

"I loved my mom, but she was weak." Maria twirled a ring she wore around her forefinger. "It was a long time ago, and not important now." She jumped to her feet, the long sleeveless dress swaying.

Riley forged ahead despite Maria's reluctance to discuss her family. It was a sad truth that in cases of abductions, it was often the other parent, or a family member.

"What about Dante's father?"

"He doesn't have one. He has me." Maria patted her heart.

"Biologically impossible, unless you are telling me that you had invitro? Which all can be verified, Maria."

Maria's lower lip jutted. "It doesn't matter!" She left Dante's room, heading for the kitchen.

"It might," Riley said to Maria's back. She still needed to search the house and call Matthew. Barnes.

They reached the island counter. Maria was on one side with the sink and cabinets and Riley on the other. She stared hard at her friend—this was urgent. "Who is Dante's father?"

"Dante doesn't know. The…sperm donor…doesn't care. I want to keep it that way."

"Coby?"

"He's never asked, and I never volunteered."

What a secret to have kept for all these years.

"Maria, please? You must let me help you find Dante which means that you have got to be honest with me. I will do my best to keep your secret."

"I know, I'm trying." Maria kept patting the phone in her apron pocket.

Try harder, Riley wanted to say. "Could your cousins have something to do with it?"

"No," Maria said, adamant. "They're bugging me about something else. They want me to return to Brooklyn, but I won't ever go back."

"Stay here by the sink," Riley instructed. "I'll check the rest of the house."

Tears gushed from Maria's eyes as reality set in. Someone evil had broken in and taken her beautiful, sweet son.

"We will get him back," Riley assured her friend, a woman as broken as any mother can be. She knew that it was not going to be easy since it was the Fourth of July, a holiday weekend, and she and Matthew were the only police on the island. They needed Barnes here, ASAP.

Riley slowly canvassed the house glad it was only three bedrooms and one story. The back door had been busted off its hinges. Her belly knotted when she saw two sets of footprints—one little boy size, the other, adult. Probably male, size ten. Unfortunately, the most average size foot for a man in America. She used her phone to snap pictures. The backyard was empty. She'd need to question the neighbors to see if they saw anything, but the homes here were on half-acre lots, making it unlikely. She might have Rosita do the questioning while she and Matthew made the calls and activated the search.

Maria hadn't listened to Riley's directive to stay put and joined her at the back door. When she saw it broken, she screamed.

"Hush, now." Riley dropped her phone to catch Maria, who sank to her knees. They hit the ground hard.

"Who has my baby?" Maria sobbed.

Riley held the woman with compassion. A minute or two now would hopefully give Maria the strength to continue what might be an awful outcome.

She helped Maria to her feet, grabbed her own phone, and walked her to the kitchen.

Filling another full glass of water from the door in the

fridge, she handed it to Maria. "Drink this. Take a few breaths, and then you have got to be straight with me."

Maria gulped the water. "Dante. Why come back here?" The woman raced down the hall toward Dante's bedroom.

Riley caught up and blocked her from entering. "What is it?"

Maria sobbed helplessly. "Whoever took him wanted him to have his special things."

Riley shook her head. "Maria. That sounds like someone who knows him. It's what a parent might do."

Maria stared at Riley with a quivering chin, her eyes wide in denial. "It's impossible."

"Who is his dad?"

Maria picked up a stuffed lion and shuffled back to the kitchen. "I can't say. You're on the wrong track."

"Do you have anybody you'd consider an enemy? Your uncles? Cousins?"

Maria straightened and Riley realized she'd touched a nerve.

Impatient, Riley curled her hands into fists. "Give me names, Maria. For God's sake, we need the truth if you ever want to see your boy alive again."

"Of course, I do!" Maria turned her back and replaced her water with wine, holding the stuffed lion like a baby. "It started in high school." She drank and tipped her glass in Riley's direction. At the shake of her head, Maria poured more into her own, slopping a little over the edge.

"Yes?" Riley encouraged, hoping for answers at last.

"I thought he was so romantic. And so sexy, the way Italian men can be, with deep brown eyes and swarthy skin. I'd hoped he would get me out of Brooklyn and show me the world. We talked about Italy. We dreamed about being different than our families."

"Who?"

"Gino Ferraro, the bastard."

Riley typed in the name on her notes function. "Why so vehement?"

"He was so controlling—ten times worse than my uncle. I had to get away before he trapped me in a life I didn't want. I escaped from Gino when Mom died. We'd been together since I was seventeen and he bullied me for years. He thought he owned me, but I escaped him and never looked back."

Maria gulped a mouthful of wine, her hand shaking.

"If he knew I was carrying his baby when I left, he would have killed me."

CHAPTER FOUR

Riley studied Maria, taking note of the fluttering pulse at her throat, looking for signs of dishonesty as she attempted to piece the timeline together.

"When did you see Gino last? I mean, you escaped twenty years ago, and Dante is only six. What happened?" Riley hated to poke holes in her friend's story, but it was her job to find Dante through every possible means.

"I miscarried. Gino never found out that I was pregnant. I wanted that baby even knowing it was his—I just didn't want that life. I was terrified that he'd find out." A remnant of fear tinged her words.

"I'm sorry about the miscarriage." Riley mulled this information over. She'd been hoping for a current enemy. "That was a very long time ago, Maria. Did you ever return?"

"Yes. Once a few years before my dad's funeral. He'd been very ill for a while; figured it was my duty and that I might never see him again. You weren't on the island yet, Riley."

"This might sound cold, but did you cut him out of your life when you fled, like you did with Gino?" Riley understood erasing a person from your life to save your child—Kyra's dad was not involved at all, and she had no regrets.

"Something like that." Maria sipped her merlot. Her cheeks were pink with emotion. "Dad wasn't the best husband or father. Had his own set of troubles, including the mob."

The mob? Riley was aware of the long arms of the mafia network throughout New York--among other places. "The restaurant. Were they squeezing him for protection?"

"It was a family-owned pizzeria. Besides the money, they threatened his life if he didn't do certain things. They pretty much owned him, and he was too immersed to run away as I did." Maria hiccupped. "It wasn't really his fault. He wasn't raised to think independently. All he wanted was to manage the pizza joint in Brooklyn and provide for us."

A familiar motive for doing the wrong thing, Riley thought. "And your mom. Did she know about the mob connections?"

"Poor sweet mom. I believe she did." Maria peeked through her long red curls. "She died young from a broken heart." She sniffed and Riley put a comforting hand over hers. "I was turning twenty in a few weeks, and just found out that I was pregnant. I knew I had to leave before I fell into that same trap. With Mom gone, I had my chance."

Riley had been blessed with amazing parents, but she was no stranger to an abusive family dynamic because of her career. Many kids stayed and continued the cycle of crime and abuse because it was all they knew. "It must have been difficult to walk away."

"Not really. I'd skipped college and was working at the pizza parlor, hanging out with Gino. He made fun of me for wanting my own restaurant away from Brooklyn. It pissed me off. He was getting in over his head and wanted to drag me down with him."

Riley studied Maria. The clock was ticking fast, but she

sensed that if she pushed Maria too hard, she'd refuse to talk at all. "You had a tough life but you're a survivor, for sure."

"Dad didn't want me to go but didn't stop me either. Had enough problems without me and Gino adding to it."

"You were extremely brave. It must have been difficult starting a new life here with nobody you knew."

"That was the appeal," Maria said. "I didn't want Gino to find me. I never told my dad or my uncle where I lived."

Riley checked her phone but there was no word from Matthew or Rosita. Exhaling, she dug for more information. "You have no siblings in Brooklyn?"

"No. Only my cousins. They do everything my uncle says… they'll inherit the family pizza business. I don't want any part of it." Maria's eyes narrowed with fury. "They think I'm the loser!"

"What are their names?"

"Does it matter?"

"Everything matters from here on out. Names please?"

"Marco Esposito and Ricky Russo."

"Thank you." Riley glanced at the time on her watch. Three in the afternoon. "Until Dante's home every detail is more important than you think. So, what can you tell me? Did Gino ever find out about your miscarriage?"

"Yeah." Maria finished the wine and put the glass down. Her stranglehold on the poor lion tightened. "Gino surprised me as I was leaving my father's bedside at the hospital. He said he wanted to apologize." She shook her head. "What BS. He would never forgive me, and I didn't care. I was glad he was no longer in my life."

"Did you make peace with your dad before you left?"

"I tried but it wasn't easy, no matter what he said. Done is done."

"Funny how people always want to come clean when death is near."

Maria looked directly at Riley, holding her gaze. "As soon as

I left Dad's room, Gino maneuvered me into the empty chapel, asking about his kid, saying that my cousins told him I was pregnant when I'd disappeared. There's a reason I don't trust them." Maria shivered in spite of the heat. "The jerk laughed and told me he'd teach our boy the family business. He was an enforcer in the mob." She put the lion down with a shaking hand. "At that moment I was glad that I'd lost the baby, that I'd gotten free. Do you understand? He had no hold over me. He didn't believe me when I explained about the miscarriage. He accused me of lying to him and then slugged me in the jaw."

Riley hid a gasp. Violence never got easy to hear about.

"I shoved Gino back and he tripped, hitting the wooden pew hard. I ran and hid until I saw him leave. He had his hand to the back of his head. I hoped I'd hurt him. I snuck out of the hospital to my rental car and swore I'd never see them again." Maria peered out to the kitchen table and the bouquet of fresh flowers in the center. "He wanted to punish me. Pathetic son of a bitch. He was so angry that I'd gotten away from him when Mom died." She met Riley's gaze. "I was trash to him, and he wanted me to know it."

"Did you report this?" Riley the cop asked the question but as a friend she already knew the answer. *No.* There wasn't always justice in this world, though Riley did her best to change that where she could.

Maria shook her head. "Escaping him was enough for me. I never want Dante to have any connections to my past. Nobody in Brooklyn knows about him. With Dad dead, I have no reason to return—no matter how many times my cousins ask."

Riley rounded the counter and hugged Maria hard. "Kyra's dad was abusive when he drank. For some reason I thought it was okay because I'd married him, and I was embarrassed that I'd chosen so poorly. My fault."

Maria's gaze filled with empathy.

"But when he broke Kyra's arm, I left. I understand what you are feeling better than you might know. Abuse is wrong. You were smart to get away." Riley hoped that now Maria would be honest and open up completely. No more secrets. "Who is Dante's father?"

Riley's patience was rewarded. A look of chagrin crossed Maria's face. "As you know, I've lived here for twenty years, and I was always careful to cover my tracks from Gino and what family I have left. Seven years ago, I was completely enamored with a very sensual man the same age as me. An artist. Free-thinker. Traveled a lot."

"How did you two meet?" Riley asked casually to encourage her talking.

"Sounds corny but we met on a dating site and really hit it off. It was nice to flirt and feel like a queen. He treated me so nicely, and we'd see each other a couple of times a week. After about a month I invited him here to my place and we made love. More than once. Condoms really do break." Maria gave a sheepish shrug. "I wanted to tell him that I was pregnant in person or on the phone, but he didn't return my calls. Finally, I texted with a cryptic message that it was important news with a stork emoji. When he didn't respond I got angry and called again. A woman answered and told me to never call back."

"Oh no!" Riley said, feeling Maria's pain.

"That was the end of our budding friendship. I never saw him again," Maria said. "I didn't even put his name on the birth certificate preferring to leave it blank. Dante has me, and that is enough. Coby has been understanding and doesn't press me for information I don't want to share."

"Could this guy have taken Dante?" Riley asked.

"Nathan White? Not a chance. He's one of the good guys, you know? Would walk an old lady across the road—one of those." Maria released a sigh, her cheeks red. "Unless that was all an act." Embarrassed by her mistake, she chewed her bottom lip. "How could I have been so naïve?

Riley touched her hand. "This is not on you, it's on him. You were just a young woman in love."

"I know, but I still feel like a fool. Coby better never turn out like that." Maria rubbed her hands together. "It's hard for me to really trust someone, you know?"

"I get that. Until Kyra is out of college, she and my mom will be my primary concern." Riley cleared her throat. "So, the last time you were in Brooklyn was for the funeral?"

Maria's face paled. "Yes, but I was on the lookout for Gino every minute. I can't thank you enough for taking care of Dante while I was gone. You see now how important it was."

Kyra had cared for Dante like he was her own…the fact that he was missing was tearing her daughter up. "What about those cousins? You said your family didn't know about Dante. That you covered your tracks."

"I saw my uncle and the family briefly at Dad's funeral. I told them I was married and lived in Portland."

"That was risky, being so close to here."

Maria snickered; her mouth sly. "Oregon. As far from here as possible,"

"Smart thinking. They have no reason to contact you, do they?"

"No, they don't." Maria's brow furrowed. "Perhaps it has something to do with Dad's inheritance."

Was the mob behind this? Maria's father's death was so recent it had to be the answer. Matthew sent her a text with a question mark. Riley focused on Maria, very aware of the need for speed.

"My cousins are idiots," Maria said. "They both suck up to Gino. Hang out with the same crowd but don't get the same respect, at least that's what Dad told me. Wannabe mobsters, which is beyond pathetic."

"I will need their contact information and anything else you can think of. What if they have Dante?"

Maria waved her hand in dismissal. "Marco and Ricky are such sissies that I can't see them doing anything that might actually be dangerous. Unless to show Gino how clever they are? Or the gangsters they want to impress?" Her eyes grew wide as she realized she'd been dodging them. "Ohmygod."

"Could be control. Of you? I don't know." Riley studied her friend. "It's important."

Maria called the number back but there was no answer, and no offer to leave a voice message. A knock sounded on Maria's front door, and she rushed to answer it, with Riley right behind. She was relieved to see Coby and removed her hand from the holster of her gun.

Maria pulled Coby in and gave him a big hug. "Has something happened?" she cried. At the shake of his head, she collapsed in sobs. He held her tenderly.

"We hadn't heard from you, so I ran here when my group finished the grid," Coby said. "Any news?"

Maria flung her arm to the side. "Someone was in Dante's bedroom. They broke into the house from the backyard and took him."

"What?"

Riley met his gaze. "No one has been in contact, but Dante's new clothes and a few toys were taken. It's as if they cared."

"They?" Coby paled beneath his summer tan.

"I don't know who!" Maria wrung her hands. "It can't be my cousins. It just can't be."

Riley led the couple to Maria's sofa. "Why don't you put your heads together and create a list of people who might have a reason to take Dante."

"Nobody!" Maria said immediately.

"Next, make a second list of all your local friends on the island. I'll be in touch, but I've got to make a missing child report and call the chief." Her personal to-do list was growing as she raced the clock.

"Why the friends list?" Coby asked.

"To ask if they saw anything suspicious," Riley explained. She glanced at the grief-stricken couple and softened her voice. "Please be very careful and limit your movements, all right? I'll need a team to dust for prints and being a holiday, I don't know how long that might take."

"You can stay with me at my place," Coby hugged Maria's shoulder. "What do you know so far?"

Maria shrugged. "Not much, but I was telling Riley everything that might help with the investigation. We're just gathering information at this moment."

This was every parent's nightmare. "I have phone numbers to share for immediate counseling, Maria, that I'll send from the station. Right now, I've got to inform Chief Barnes, if Matthew hasn't already. The FBI. And alert the local folks that we have a child abduction. Also, we need to know where Gino Ferraro is along with the Brooklyn cousins."

"Cousins? Who the heck is Gino?" Coby looked from Riley to Maria.

Maria lowered her head. "A terrible man that I dated when I was very young. He's not a good person."

"Why would he have Dante?" Coby asked in confusion.

Riley raised her hand to put that line of thought to a halt. "We don't know who has Dante, all right? We don't want to assume anything." She was feeling the pressure as only she and Matthew were the officers on the island, with Rosita's invaluable help. She sent Matt a text saying that she was on the way to the station.

"I don't want to stay with you, Coby," Maria said softly, stroking his face. "What if Dante comes home and I'm not here?"

"You need to stay, Maria," Riley said. "Just be careful what you touch. Call me if you hear from your cousins, or Gino, or anybody else."

Maria held hands with her boyfriend. "Find Dante, please, Riley!"

"Be sure to keep Dante's bedroom closed, all right? We want to avoid any more contamination."

"We will," Coby promised.

Riley left via the front door with a nod and hurried to her SUV, dialing Matthew as she drove to the station.

"How's it going?" he asked immediately.

"Where are you?" she asked over him.

"Still at the park," Matt answered. "Rosita has volunteers widening their search to the other part of the island and the woods. Dante is no longer in Mackabee Park, I'd stake my badge on it."

"I know." Riley drew a breath. "He was brought to his home. The back door lock was busted and some of his clothes and toys were taken."

"What the hell?"

Riley sucked in a breath at the goodhearted Matthew's vehemence. "I know. It's time to call in the FBI to help us search. Barnes, first, of course. Let's meet at the station, all right?"

"Yeah. This really sucks." Matthew vented with a second, more colorful curse. "Who would do such a thing?"

"I don't know, but I've got some answers from Maria that I'll feel better sharing in person, rather than over the phone." Maria's secrets were very personal in nature. Not just a broken condom, but the mob connections.

"Sure. See you."

Riley ended the call, and dialed Kyra. "Hey sweetie!"

"Did you find Dante?" Kyra asked.

"Not yet. Is Nana there?"

"We are staying on the blanket like you told us." Kyra sounded pouty. "Everyone else has joined the search parties."

The phone shuffled and then Susan said, "I'm here."

"We'll have to cancel the dinner plans for today," Riley said.

"It's going to be a long night. Dante was brought back to his house, where the back door was broken. The abductor took some of his clothes. His favorite pajamas." Stating that fact made her head spin. "We're going to call in the FBI. We will find him."

Kyra, having listened to that awful news, started to cry. Her mom said, "I called Wyatt. He hasn't seen Dante either but will keep an eye out for him."

"Thanks, Mom," Riley said. She'd need to get the manifest of customers who had traveled to the island in the past two days on the ferry. Although some came by their own boat which would need to be checked at the marina. "Listen, I don't know how late I am going to be, but I want you guys to be as calm as possible about this. If it makes sense for you to contact Rosita and help with a search, then do that, but just let me know where you are and who you are with, all right?"

"Really?" Kyra's tears stopped and her tone turned hopeful.

"We can do that," Susan said. "Riley, don't worry about us. You take care of yourself and do what you do best. Get the bad guy."

Her mother's faith in her abilities had never wavered, no matter what happened. "Let's stay in contact, even with just a text. Love you both," Riley said. She hung up, torn between going to Wyatt's for the list or the station to call Barnes.

As much as she wanted to turn toward the ferry, she stayed the course and parked at Sandpiper Bay Police Department, next to Matthew's sedan.

He opened the door for her, his expression grim. "I suppose you've done this lots of times, but I haven't. This is my first actual kidnapped kid, and it is terrifying."

Riley grasped his upper arm. "I've only been on three kidnapping cases—two were the other noncustodial parent. The child was fine both times. Not so with the third. She was found floating in a pond."

"Good God."

"It's not easy, Matthew. But," she urged him inside the office and locked the door behind them, "I have the name of Dante's biological father. He hasn't been involved with the parenting but should be checked out. Nathan White."

She filled him in on what Maria had shared with her, asking unnecessarily of course, for him to be tactful with the information. "Gino Ferraro is not Dante's father, but he was very vindictive with Maria. Controlling." She quickly updated him on the turn of events, the miscarriage, years later hooking up with a man who was already married. A broken condom? Seriously?

Matthew made a pot of coffee. "Want me to put his name in the system?"

"Yes, Gino for sure. Nathan White. Give me a minute." Riley dialed Barnes again. Where was he? She eyed the time. He had fifteen minutes, or she would have to call the FBI without alerting him first, which would tick him off. "Do you know his daughter's home number?"

"No, but I bet Rosita will. She's a natural with people and so good at getting things organized, like the search at the park."

Riley nodded. "Agreed. Let's find out what she wants to do."

"I can't even find out what *you* want," Matthew grumped. "You staying on the island, or heading off to a new adventure?"

"Not the right time, Matt. We'll have this conversation once we have Dante home. Right now, Kyra is excited to be offered a last-minute trip with other art students and is leaving in a few days to Paris."

"This is not a bad place to live," Matthew said.

Riley arched her brow. "A child has just been kidnapped."

"Usually," Matthew amended. "No place is perfect."

She placed the landline in the center of the breakroom table and put the phone on Speaker, dialing Barnes. No answer. Using her cell phone, she sent Rosita a text to see what other phone numbers might help locate their chief. Wife, or daughter.

"While we wait for Barnes, I'll try Wyatt."

"What for?" Matt asked. He wrote down Gino Ferraro. Nathan White. Maria Catalina. Dante Catalina.

"To see if Gino Ferraro was on the ferry at any time this past week." Riley dialed. Again, the phone rang and rang, but then the captain's gruff voice answered, "Sandpiper Bay Ferry Depot, Captain Wyatt speaking."

"Wyatt! It's Riley."

"Have you found Dante?"

"No. I was hoping to see your manifest for today and yesterday, to start. Maybe longer."

"Damn it." Wyatt knew Maria and Dante well. "Let me forward it to your email."

"Thanks." Riley glanced at Matthew, his strain to find answers reflected on his face. Impatient she asked, "Uh, soon?"

Her email pinged.

"Done," Wyatt said.

"You're the best," Riley replied, ending the call. She got up and went with Matthew into her office, opening the email on her desktop computer.

Her cell phone chimed again, and she handed it to Matthew.

"Rosita sent his wife's cell phone number," Matthew said his voice loud and excited over her shoulder. "And the daughter's too. Want me to call the Mrs.?"

"Hang on first."

She opened the attachment from Wyatt and read through the list, searching for Gino Ferraro.

"No Gino aboard the ferry today," she said. Her stomach rose in her throat and lodged there as she found something else of interest. Swallowing hard she said, "Oh my God—call Barnes again and keep dialing any possible number you have until you get his butt on the phone."

"What?"

"No Gino Ferraro but there was a Marco Esposito on the

ferry yesterday morning." Riley stood and clenched her fists, letting the emotions come. She stopped the roller coaster, ending with the determination to find the man who'd been a fool to cause trouble on her island.

"Who is that?" Matthew plopped in her chair to read the screen better.

"Cousin. Maria told me about them, Ricky and Marco. I'll fill you in later."

Riley paced behind Matthew, her thoughts spinning wild.

"Why is that a big deal?" Matthew asked.

"Maria is under the impression that her cousins don't know where she lives. But they've been in touch. The family pizza business in Brooklyn has been supported by the mob and her dad just died with a possible inheritance. Money sounds like a good motive to me."

Matthew swiveled in her chair. "The mob? Can this get any worse?"

CHAPTER FIVE

Riley moaned. "I'm so furious with Maria that I'm ready to put her behind bars." She glanced at Matthew. "You better handle her yourself, since I was with her for a couple of hours practically begging her to speak the truth."

"You filled me in, and I thought she'd given you a thorough report, as much as she could anyway."

"What if the cousins were blowing up her phone to tell her they had Dante? I doubt that they'd want him, but they might want the money Maria inherited."

"Blackmail. Of course." Matthew leaned against the wall; arms crossed. "Reassuring in a way. They won't harm him, just keep him safe until we, the good guys, find them, get the boy, and put them away for a long, long time." His lips twitched. "Should have Dante by tomorrow morning."

Riley threw a pencil at his head. "You expect a parade or something?"

"I wouldn't go that far. But damn, it would feel good."

"Hate to burst your bubble but we're a long way from recovering Dante. We have no idea where to look."

"Never seen you so negative before. What crawled up your ass?"

"Reality. How did they find him and get him off the island with so many people around? And if they think Maria knows where the money is, they will be waiting and watching."

Before Matthew could answer, Riley pointed at the phone. "Get a hold of Barnes, would you? We don't want to be the fools who let that sweet boy be a pawn for the cousins or the mob. Got it?"

"Yeah. I'll give it another shot."

Riley left a message for Maria, who wasn't answering either of her phones. She hated to feel like she was being played.

Their hands were tied until they talked with Chief Barnes. "Five minutes, or I am contacting the FBI myself," Riley said.

Matthew got up from her desk, nodding at the calendar with July 15th circled. Her email chimed another message from the Phoenix Police Department. Her partner's eyes rounded. "I don't understand…"

"Officer Marcy Kendricks would like me back in Phoenix and has offered some tempting perks. Just forget you saw that," Riley suggested. "I am."

"How can I?" Matthew dialed Barnes's daughter's phone number. No answer. "Where are these people?"

Riley's cell phone rang, and she answered on Speaker. "It's Barnes! Hello, Chief. We have an emergency; Dante Catalina has been kidnapped."

"Whoa! Slow down. I was in the longest most boring movie known to man. Damn it. Say that again?"

Matthew updated him from the moment of Dante's disappearance until the most current information to date. "What would you like us to do, Chief?"

"Calm down," Barnes said. "I'll call the FBI. Have Rosita come in from the field and get her reports to me. Matthew and Riley, I want to know everything about Maria and Dante from social security numbers to dental records. Standby at the station until I call."

Barnes hung up and Riley and Matthew exchanged relieved glances. Matthew stepped out of Riley's office. "I'll call Rosita."

"I'll dig into Maria's past." Vindication for holding back the full truth. It didn't feel wrong. It was them against the clock to find Dante.

Thirty minutes later, Rosita entered the station. "Hey, guys." She paused by Nancy's front desk and Matthew and Riley left their offices to greet her.

"Good to see you," Matthew said. "And thanks for the phone numbers—we finally reached Barnes and he contacted the FBI. He wants us to send him everything we have."

Riley quickly updated Rosita on the broken back door and that Dante's abductor had brought him home to retrieve clothes and a couple of toys.

"That's very strange," Rosita said. "Why would they do something that risky?"

"That's the million-dollar question," Riley said with some heat.

Rosita raised a brow.

"Barnes has asked us to send him all of our reports. Your notes from your search will be important." Riley sighed. "I'm about ready to send what I have to his email."

Rosita shook her head. "You can put me to work. Assemble what you have, and I'll fax it to him."

"Thanks Rosita, what would we do without you?"

Matthew grinned. "Nothing but stale donuts?"

"Funny." Riley swatted his arm. "So, we best get busy and have all our ducks in a row. The chief should be calling back any minute with news regarding the FBI. What do *you* need, Rosita?"

"Our volunteer groups are still eager to help. I have their contact information and they know to call if they see anything."

Rosita was in her civilian clothes but had put on a Sandpiper Bay police department baseball cap. "Is there anything I can tell them to give them hope?"

Riley leaned her hip against the front counter. "It has to be kind of vague but maybe just say that we have new information which needs to be verified before making any big announcements? That we believe Dante is still alive and will be home soon."

"Why would anybody kidnap Dante…is this Gino from Maria's past? What does he want?"

Rosita's voice was shaky, and Riley felt sorry that she couldn't give her more positive news. "We are not sure as they haven't made contact." Not that Maria was fessing up to, anyway. "If the abductors are still on this island we will find them, don't worry."

Rosita drew in a long breath and exhaled slowly. "None of my crew saw anything suspicious. Darren's either."

"We don't know who or why someone took Dante," Riley clarified. Jumping to conclusions didn't make for solid policework. "We know the Catalina house was broken into, and that Marco Esposito, a man from her past, was on the ferry yesterday. Discovered this from Wyatt's roster."

"All right," Rosita said.

"I can't say more right now." Riley cleared her throat.

It was difficult to bury Maria's story of control and abuse by Gino Ferraro since he wasn't on the island, but her cousin was. Maybe both of them but Marco for sure. How had he found her?

Matthew's office phone rang, and he rushed to answer it, waving at Rosita.

"Thanks, Riley," Rosita said. "I'll inform the troops to stand down for now. Want me to work tonight?"

"No, but thanks for the offer. The FBI will be involved because it's a child kidnapping, and Barnes is calling in some favors. He'll be here soon. We'll keep you in the loop as much as possible, Rosita. It's going to be a long and busy night. Get some rest; we might need you here tomorrow even though it's a Sunday."

"Of course," Rosita said. "I will work around the clock to help find our Dante."

"Can you give me all of your notes from the search, to add to my report to Barnes?" Riley asked.

Rosita pulled her notes and the maps she'd used for the search from her backpack and gestured to her office. "I'll do it now. This way the FBI will know where we've looked already. I hope we didn't destroy any clues."

"I saw your instructions to the team leaders, and you did just fine. Thank you. You've been a great help." The civilian officer went into her office, moving quickly.

Riley discovered Matt in his office on the phone, once again talking to the chief. She sat opposite him.

Matthew swung his chair around and nodded to Riley. When the conversation ended, he let out a huge sigh of relief.

"Don't keep me hanging. What did he say?"

"The FBI has a team of experts who work specifically on missing and exploited children. They have bases all through the county and the nearest one is right here in Portland. He knows Special Agent Charlie Craig. Everyone calls him C.C."

"Go on," Riley urged. Portland, Maine was a good-sized city along the coast, population around 68000, about twice the size of Bangor.

"Chief called him and told him what we know." Matt ran a hand through his short rust-colored hair. "Help is on the way and Barnes will be here by six."

"I had a chance to work with the FBI's Field Office in Phoenix. Professional. Dedicated. They know their stuff and have great success in bringing the missing children home." Riley leaned back in her chair and smiled for the first time after her daughter's frantic call. Had it only been five hours ago? Felt like a hundred.

"So, let's get busy and uncover everything we can on this Gino Ferraro creep." Matthew rubbed his hands together. "It's almost too bad that the special agents will find him first because I'd really like to get my hands on him."

"If Gino has Dante, then yes, I agree," Riley said. "But I think we need to check out this Marco Esposito." Maria still hadn't called back.

Riley left Matthew in his office and returned to hers to double-check the appropriate paperwork for a missing child. Dante Catalina. She already had the information from Maria earlier and reached for her notes: Dante's birthdate, hair color, eye color, age. Height. Small mark on his chin. Social security number. Dental records were left blank. As a kid he didn't have a dentist yet.

He was so young. The sooner he was rescued and returned home the less scar tissue the child would have. There were amazing therapists on hand to help the healing process from the terror of his abduction.

She couldn't think about the alternative, where he didn't come home.

Rosita knocked on Riley's open office door. "Hey. Are you finished?"

"Not yet," Riley said. "Why don't you just fax the chief your report without waiting for me…it's taking a little longer. Thanks again for your help."

"Sure. No problem." Rosita's brown eyes grew sad, and she showed Riley her cell phone. "I will have it on all night if you need me."

"Thank you!"

Rosita left.

Riley compiled everything she had and sent it to Barnes, though Maria Catalina's background had some holes. She didn't want to hold the FBI up for the information on Dante. Riley had a sinking feeling that Maria was hiding something important. Did she want to keep her father's inheritance, even if the money was dirty?

A few minutes later, Matthew leaned against her open doorframe with a printout in his hand. "This Gino dude is bad news. Lots of petty crime but he was even in jail around the same time frame as Maria's arrival in Sandpiper Bay. Coincidence?"

"Maria was running from him," Riley explained. "He'd been promoted to an enforcer for the mob in Brooklyn."

"Damn! If he did this, I hope he rots in hell." Matthew gritted his teeth and ran a hand through his ginger hair making it stand on end.

Raised on the island, Matthew had been sheltered from the cruelty that existed beyond this usually safe, friendly paradise. It was a hard blow for him to accept.

"Matt, if Gino is behind the kidnapping, he will be punished, and Dante will be back home soon with his mom." She gestured to the long list of Gino's crimes in Matthew's hand. "It makes me sick too, but I'm more used to the evil in this world. All we can do is arrest these assholes and lock them away, one bastard at a time."

Matthew chuckled. "Unlike you to swear like that. Shocking, Miss Riley."

"Sorry, but I usually keep it inside. Don't want Kyra to hear my garbage mouth."

"I'll keep your secret, I promise." Matthew cleared his throat. "So, what else have you learned about Maria's past? Anymore skeletons in the closet?"

Riley's nape tingled at the phrase. "Yeah, actually. Look at this." She'd entered Maria Catalina into the search bar thinking the name would pop right up. She'd never had a reason to ask Maria for ID. "I can't find a Maria Catalina who lived in Brooklyn at that time. Maria told me she'd never married though she's had previous relationships before meeting Coby."

"Guess at her age, it's perfectly normal. What about her cousins?"

Riley switched to a different document. "The cousins have had a few stints in the county jail. Selling drugs to minors, car theft, robbery. No weapons at any of the crimes. They were released early for good behavior. Marco Esposito and Ricky Russo are petty criminals who never use violence, hence short prison time. Marco Esposito paid cash for his ticket and from his record he never hurts his victims. With that in mind it's probable he won't touch a hair on Dante's head."

"That makes me feel a little less sick to my stomach," Matthew said.

"We need way more information for that Nathan guy." Riley reached for her cell phone. "I'm going to give Maria another call. She's either passed out or avoiding me."

"Let her know that the chief has contacted the FBI's special unit," Matthew said. "Chief Barnes will be here around six."

Riley dialed Maria's number and the distraught mother answered right away. "Did you find him?" she gasped.

A pang shot through her as she realized Maria was living on hope and had misconstrued the nature of the call. "I'm deeply sorry, but no. We do have some good news though. Chief Barnes will be here soon, and he's called the FBI unit whose job is to find missing children. They should arrive around the same time as Barnes. I worked with another branch when I lived in Phoenix, and they have an amazing record of finding children within forty-eight hours." Riley sucked in a breath before continuing, "Maria, I have more questions."

"Of course. Anything."

Riley could hear her sniffling and choking on her tears. Trying desperately to hold on.

"This is kind of strange," Riley said softly, "since we've

known each other for the past year so well. But what is your legal name?"

Maria paused.

Riley continued, "I put Maria Catalina into the database."

"You're running a background check on me?" Maria sounded shocked.

"No! Not that, but…" Riley hesitated at the panic in her friend's voice. "Would that be a problem?"

"No. It wouldn't. *I've* never been in trouble with the law."

Riley sensed more to it than that. "Maria, would you like to come to the station so we can talk, face to face? This is not about your past as much as it is about finding Dante."

"It's okay, Riley. I know that you're not trying to pry."

Riley drummed her fingers to the desktop. "Maria, the FBI will ask direct questions and demand answers. Their job is to find your son as fast as possible. What is your legal name?"

Maria sighed. "Sorry. I probably should have told you this before at the house."

Riley eyed the ceiling in frustration. The time for secrets was over. "Tell me now so I can relate it to the FBI."

"I was born Maria Elena Russo." Riley typed that name in, followed by Bronx and Brooklyn, hoping something in the public road would show Maria was telling the truth. "Mom's maiden name was Catalina. When she was dying, she made me promise to leave the New York area and start over. She had some money hidden away and gave it to me. But you know all that from earlier."

News clips showed Russo Pizzeria being related to the Brooklyn mob. Maria's uncle, Alphonso Esposito. Cousins Marco Esposito and Ricky Russo.

"If it weren't for my dad's dying wishes, I wouldn't have even visited. They corrupted him and it poisoned everything he touched."

"You knew that Gino Ferraro had been to jail?"

"Yes. Petty stuff."

"What else can you tell me about him?"

"Nothing new since our previous conversation! How is this helping you to find my son?"

"Did you know your dad was doing something illegal?"

Maria blew out a breath. "We had a nice house, and cars—better than most in the neighborhood. I was a teenager, but I heard some rumors and laughed them off."

"What does Marco Esposito want from you?"

"Ricky and Marco are stupid goons, it's Gino who's running this show. Gino hasn't been in touch, but I'd wager he thinks I've taken the mob's money and he wants it back! I don't have it. How can I give what I don't have?"

"When did he last make contact?"

"Gino? Two weeks ago. Told me to get my ass back to Brooklyn, or I would be sorry."

"Why didn't you mention this before?"

"I forgot about it until now. I texted him with the succinct message to go to hell and never contact me again."

"And did he?"

"I don't know because I blocked his number. I almost had done that to Marco." Maria wailed with remorse. "What if Marco was trying to tell me that he has my son? He won't answer the phone now."

Riley's fingers flew over the keyboard to get beyond just the surface information. The three of them were something else. They'd each done jail time. Slicked-back black hair, gold fillings in their teeth, facial tattoos, as well as arms and necks with snakes. "Are you sure that they don't know about Dante?"

Maria sighed. "Positive."

"Maria." Riley wished that she was able to deliver this news face to face. "Marco Esposito arrived in Sandpiper Bay yesterday, via the ferry."

"No!" Maria repeated the word over and over.

"Chief Barnes will be here," Riley checked the time on the wall clock, five-thirty, "by six. He has contacted the FBI. They'll want to speak with you and search Dante's room for clues."

"Clues?"

"Fingerprints. If the person has been to jail, theirs will be on file."

"That's good news then," Maria said. "They all did time. Where is Ricky? He's the scariest of all. Has a mean streak that he doesn't show often, but it's always simmering just beneath the surface. Him and Marco are attached at the hip. I need to call! I have all their numbers. Or Uncle Alphonso!"

"Maria, wait!" Riley was afraid that the woman might act rashly when this situation needed to be controlled as much as possible.

"Why not? I have to know!"

"You need to give me their numbers at once, and let the FBI take over. Listen to me. This is extremely important. It could make the difference between getting Dante returned untouched, or not."

Riley could hear her gasp and make moaning sounds. Coby came on the line. "What's going on?"

"Maria has Gino's, Ricky's, and Marco's phone numbers. I need them right now."

"I'll get them for you."

While she was on hold, Riley told Matthew what was going on. She put it on Speaker phone so they could question her together and have it recorded.

Coby returned with the requested phone numbers. They typed them into the system, not knowing if they were live numbers or burner phones.

"I'm back," Maria said. "I'm so angry at myself! I should have answered Marco because now he's ignoring me."

"Did he leave a detailed message?" Matthew asked.

"This morning, Marco kept texting that he wanted me to

come home." Maria's voice shook. "They want to have a family conversation at the pizzeria."

"Was anybody else included in the message thread?" Riley tapped a pen to a scrap of paper.

"Just Ricky." Maria sounded calmer now. "When is the FBI coming?"

"Soon. By six or so. They'll want to collect evidence to catch who has Dante."

"Riley, can you come too, with the FBI? I won't talk to them without you there. I don't trust the law," Maria said firmly.

Considering Maria's family's history of crime, Riley understood. "If I can, I will. These are the specialists, Maria, trained to find your child fast. Is there anything else you want to tell me?"

"No. That's enough," Maria replied in a short tone.

"Fair. It's for Dante, though." If Maria was hiding anything else, it would come to light eventually. Most secrets did.

"I would do anything for my baby," Maria said. "Are folks still searching for him?"

"Rosita did a very professional job with the volunteers, and created a map of everywhere the islanders went to share with the FBI agents. Everyone wants to help." Especially Kyra.

"It'll be nighttime soon," Maria said in a throaty voice. "I want my baby home before it's dark and the fireworks start. Last year he was afraid. He needs his stuffed lion."

Riley hoped to end the conversation on a positive note as neither of them wanted to envision a different outcome. "The FBI will continue the search tonight."

"How?"

"They have special equipment and heat tracking devices. I'll see you soon, okay, Maria? If you think of anything that might help us, call right away."

"Thank you, Riley." Maria's voice cracked and she sobbed with a broken heart.

Matthew gave her a thumbs-up. "Good work," her partner

nodded in sympathy then stood and stretched. "When was the last time you ate?"

Riley was grateful for the change of subject. She was about to answer when a huge rumbling sound erupted from Matt's stomach. She laughed when hers did the same. "Must be like a sneeze," she told him. "Catchy."

CHAPTER SIX

"We got any donuts left?" Matthew left Riley's office and walked down the hall to the breakroom. He opened the fridge door, stuck his head in, and pulled out the container of dried cake donuts that had little appeal. "Mom always has a casserole in the freezer, should I give her a call?"

"By the time it's unfrozen, Barnes will be here." It was quarter to six already. Riley scoured the kitchen cabinets like a mouse looking for his last meal. She let out a whoop when she discovered Ritz crackers in the pantry and some peanut butter. "A humble feast. Should we wait for something better?"

"Hell no."

Riley opened the crackers then glanced at her hungry partner, feeling a little desperate and not liking it. "Matthew, let's use the good China so we can entertain properly."

"Nothing else will do."

She snickered. "Lucky, we have a sense of humor." Over the past months they had become more than partners but good friends. She'd miss him when they left Sandpiper Bay. If they left.

After putting the meager supplies on the table, she gave the jar of Jiffy to Matthew to crack open. Riley laid the table with two plastic plates and knives.

They both swung around at the sound of several sharp knocks and the front door opening with a bang that was unlike Rosita or Chief Barnes.

"Did you lock up when Rosita left?" Riley asked Matthew.

"Yes. It's probably the chief," Matthew replied. It was six on the dot.

Matthew stood and started down the narrow hallway to the front office. Riley was right behind him. They both wore their guns on their hips. Just in case.

Chief Barnes waited at the front desk as Riley and Matthew rounded the hall from the breakroom. He was dressed in jeans with a suit jacket over a light blue polo shirt. He'd trimmed down in the past year, taking his health more seriously.

Like Matthew, he'd been dressed for a day off. He spoke to the two men behind him. "This is Officer Harper, and Officer Snider. They know how to work a crime scene." He turned to Riley and Matthew. "These men are agents with the FBI."

Riley was pleased that Barnes had brought the calvary with him but didn't care for the smug expression the men wore—especially the tall one.

The taller of the two stepped forward. Dressed in a charcoal suit, and with his no-nonsense craggy face, dark brown hair and eyes, his presence demanded respect. "I'm Agent Charlie Craig." He shook her hand, deliberately squeezing, then Matthew's outstretched grip, giving Matt's summer attire a long look. "Pleased to meet you both."

His partner, a blond giant with massive shoulders, stepped around C.C.'s broad back to shake their hands. "I'm Stephan Johansson. Call me Stephan." His shake wasn't trying to prove a point and Riley liked him better for it. His dark blue eyes looked beyond the surface level as he said to Matthew,

"Caught you on your day off, eh? Criminals don't work nine to five."

"No, they don't, but this is Saturday, and we are a little more relaxed around here." Chief Barnes defended his officer—not that he needed brownie points from Riley, but he still got them.

Agent Craig didn't loosen a muscle at the conversation. Riley wasn't sure if he was an iceberg or someone that could immediately recognize good from evil. If it were the latter, whoever had kidnapped Dante was best to hide.

"How did you guys get here?" Matthew asked. "The ferry?"

"Chopper," the Scandinavian said.

Matthew made a fist pump. "It's parked outside?" He sounded like an excited kid. The vacant lot behind the station was just big enough to land a helicopter. "Never been in one."

"You won't tonight either," Barnes replied sharply, reminding them all that it wasn't time for fun and games. "We have a job to do—find Dante Catalina."

Stephan gave Matt a shrug. "Our pilot is also an agent. Jeff Farrington. He'll be coordinating our efforts in the station from the helo, which has global satellite connected to databases all over the world."

"Yup," Agent Craig confirmed. "Right now, Jeff is putting together the state-of-the-art electronics we'll need for communication from this station. Agent Elizabeth Quinn, copilot, is a sharpshooter. Her rescue record is at the top." His face was so stern she doubted he smiled often. But in his line of work, it was no wonder. "Where can we set up shop?"

"My office," Chief Barnes suggested, opening the door so Agent Craig could see it.

"Too small," the agent drawled. "We need room to spread out our maps and laptops."

"The breakroom," both Riley and Matthew echoed each other.

Chief Barnes nodded.

Stephan put his hand on the front door. "I'll go get some of the equipment."

"I'll unlock the back door for you," Riley offered. "It's closer than having to walk around all night."

"Thanks." Riley hurried ahead as Barnes and Agent Craig discussed something in low voices. After unlocking the door to let Stephan out, she grabbed the crackers and peanut butter to put away. She was standing on her toes to stash them in the cupboard when she heard the men behind her.

"Whatchya doin?" Barnes asked.

Riley flushed as she turned to face them. "Just cleaning off the table…we were about to have some crackers for dinner. Anyone interested in sharing? We had no time for food today."

Agent Craig stepped forward and took the supplies from her hands. Was that a hint of a smile at last? "It's obvious that you've been hard at work. Jeff remembered that it was a holiday, and this island is small, so we brought six large pizzas. There's a great Italian place next to our office in Portland. Officer Snider, would you mind running out and helping Agent Quinn bring four of them in?"

"Call me Matthew," he said. "Copy that. What are you going to do with the others?"

"Save them for later." Agent Craig exhaled low. "We'll have a long night ahead."

"Think anyone might like the crackers and peanut butter?"

"It couldn't hurt, but you might need them for another day." Agent Craig put the supplies in the cupboard and closed it.

Barnes nodded at Riley. "I'm surprised you didn't order in. We're not a big place but there are options, even on a holiday."

Riley shrugged, aware of Agent Craig's gaze on her. "We were busy learning all we could about Dante so that Maria can have her son back tonight."

An awkward silence followed that remark. Riley had the feeling that Agent Craig didn't bestow respect unless it was earned. From the way he looked at Matthew's shorts and at Riley, specifically, she'd guess that he knew of her history in Phoenix.

Matt held the back door open for Stephan, passing the agent as he went to the helo. Riley heard the whir of the blades slow before the door closed.

Stephan set a heavy-duty plastic crate on the oval table in the breakroom. "Did you decide to let Matthew check out the helo?"

C.C. answered, very much a man in control, "He's getting some of the pizzas for dinner."

Stephan patted the crate of laptops and various technical devices. "Glad to share. I'm hungry enough to eat a bear."

Riley went to the cupboard next to the refrigerator and pulled out a stack of paper plates and an extra roll of paper towels. "Pizza trumps peanut butter and crackers every time. Can I help you with anything?" She turned to Barnes. "I can make copies of the report I sent you."

"Already done," Agent Craig said. "After we eat, we will divvy up duties for our task force." He placed his hand on Stephan's shoulder. "Stephan here has razor-sharp vision, and he can see things in the dark that the rest of us would miss. Jeff is tech savvy as well as a gifted pilot."

"What's your skill?" Riley asked.

"C.C. here is a bloodhound," Stephan replied. "He won't stop until we find Dante—alive or dead."

Barnes's nostrils flared.

"Alive," Riley said to the stern agent.

Agent Craig blinked under her direct stare. "We all bring something to the table. What do you have?"

"Experience with previous kidnappings," Riley said firmly. "In Phoenix." Would he bring up her shameful dismissal?

"Let's get movin'," Stephan groused, breaking the tension.

"Time to bring this boy home. We need to interview the mother, see the point of entry on the house."

"Maria has asked that I be there when you question her," Riley said.

"I saw in the notes that the boy's biological father is out of the picture," Agent Craig said. "And Marco Esposito was on the ferry to Sandpiper Bay yesterday. She ran from Brooklyn and the mob—specifically Gino Ferraro."

"That's right. I haven't had the chance to dig deeper into Maria's past such as Nathan White, Ricky Russo, or her uncle, Alphonso. She is protective of her secrets," Riley said. "She was probably taught to be at an early age."

Barnes stepped between them. "You can tell us all about it while we eat. Can't do our best work without sustenance. Where is Matthew?"

Matthew arrived as if summoned by name, his face hardly visible behind the pizza boxes. He set them on the table, body glowing with excitement. "Jeff showed me the cockpit and it was so awesome. He let me sit in the chair and touch the instruments. So cool!"

"Time is of the essence." Agent Craig stepped forward with an air of disapproval.

Agent Elizabeth Quinn arrived with Agent Jeff...the redhead was five-foot-eight, and he, dark-haired and six feet. All of the officers asked to be called by their first name except for Agent Craig.

Stephan gestured to the boxes of pizza. "Dig in."

Riley devoured a piping hot slice of pepperoni and cracked open a can of fizzy water. She finished her second slice and brought out the portable whiteboard. "Should we go over what we know?"

"Sure," Jeff said. The pilot was on his third piece and finally slowing down. Next to him at the table, Elizabeth reached for a bottle of water.

"Dante Catalina, age six, has been missing since between noon and twelve-thirty." Riley printed neatly with the marker. It was seven p.m. "My daughter called me at one-fifteen, upset because she couldn't find Dante. They'd looked around the bandstand, a metal stage in the middle of the park for bands to celebrate the holiday. According to Maria, his mother, he was very excited to see the acrobats at one in the afternoon."

"Kyra was babysitting?" the chief asked.

"Not exactly. My mom and Kyra were sitting with Dante and Coby eating a hot dog. Maria said she saw him there around noon. Dante wanted to play with the bubble machine, even more than he wanted ice cream for dessert. Our population on the island is six hundred people. Because it's summer and a holiday, we had two thousand."

Stephan sucked in a breath. "Lots of tourists. Strangers."

"Exactly. Kyra looked away for a moment or two and that was the last she saw of Dante." Riley's throat thickened with emotion.

"And Susan collaborates those times?" the chief asked.

"Yes." Riley, fueled by pizza, was eager to get moving.

Barnes stood and wiped his hands on a paper towel before passing out folders to each person. Matthew, Riley, Jeff, Stephan, Elizabeth, and C.C.—Agent Craig. His face was pinched as he opened the folder.

"Your officer, Rosita Sanchez, did a very professional job with the search parties. The maps and grids are easy to follow." Agent Craig turned to the next page. "Names and phone numbers for the volunteers."

"Rosita is an asset to the team," Barnes said. "As are Matthew and Riley."

"She's on call if we want to bring her in." Riley sat down and opened the folder. "What's the plan for tonight?"

"First the interview with the mother," Stephan said. "Get

prints if there are any at the site. We didn't see that she had the kid listed on the FBI Child ID app."

"No," Riley said. "Maria is…cautious…of the law."

"It helps having the child's fingerprints and vital information at our immediate disposal to share with all law enforcement agencies." Agent Craig scrunched his napkin. "The sooner we get this ball rolling, the better the chances of finding him within the forty-eight-hour window."

Jeff briefly raised his hand and fluttered his fingers. "Elizabeth and I will be scouting from the air. The search will be cut off sooner than normal because of the fireworks. What time?"

"They start at ten," Riley answered. She hadn't been here the year before so had no idea what to expect.

"Cool!" Matthew said to Jeff. "Night vision?"

"Nah—we have a thermal imaging system that puts night vision capabilities to shame. I won't bore you with the particulars," Jeff said.

"But he could!" Elizabeth teased.

Jeff grinned. "I accept full responsibility for being a tech nerd. Bottom line is that this system will pick up movement of anything with a pulse. Body heat. Of course, in a crowd of people that becomes more difficult." He scooted back from the table.

"Mackabee Park has a band until midnight." Barnes's voice trailed off. "The marina is full of boats. It will be like searching for a needle in a haystack."

"Chief!" Matt said. "We have to find him no matter what. Failure isn't an option."

"I know. I know." Barnes looked at Agent Craig. "We work in tandem with the Coast Guard because of the busy holiday. Should I alert them of what's going on?"

"We already have," Agent Craig said.

Riley read the report. It looked good, true, but it would be better if there was a sign pointing to Dante's location. So far, the only clue was the size ten shoeprint outside Maria's house. "I'm ready when you are."

∼

AT HALF PAST SEVEN, THE TEAM SPLIT UP WITH MATTHEW AT THE station to field phone calls and emails, Jeff and Elizabeth on the chopper to begin their air search, and the other four headed to Maria's house. Riley drove with Stephan while Barnes went with Agent Craig. There were several hours of daylight left.

Riley and Stephan shared small talk, arriving seconds before Barnes and Agent Craig. He'd complimented her on her interview skills. Mob families were notoriously close-lipped. She felt bad because she considered Maria a friend but knew she had to push hard for answers.

They exited the SUV and Stephan carried a plastic storage box to the door. After a knock, Coby answered. "Hey, Riley." He nodded at the FBI agents and said another hello to Barnes. "Maria's in the kitchen."

The smell of fresh-brewed coffee made Riley's mouth water. Maria sat at the table with a box of photographs. She'd picked out the most recent—a kindergarten school photo that showed Dante's entire face rather than a candid shot. Coby put his hand on her shoulder for support.

Riley looked over the list they'd made of what he'd worn to the park—blue shorts, red, white, and blue shirt. Blue sandals with a strap. His height and weight, the dark wavy hair as well as the slight scar on his chin from falling off a bike the year before. His favorite stuffed lion sat in Dante's chair.

They had made the list of friends on the island as Riley had asked. It was a long and thorough list since Maria had lived here twenty years. Riley's family had made the cut. Next was a list of employees: Jessica, Bob, Parker. People she knew in a professional sense that Dante might be friendly with, like the delivery man, Chase.

Maria didn't write a list of enemies.

Her tears had dried; her terror subdued. Now she had hope that the experts would find her beloved son.

Riley was glad to see that Maria was still in the same sundress from earlier. It meant that the couple had done as requested and kept their movements to a minimum. Barnes and Agent Craig were right behind her and Stephan.

Maria took a calming breath and greeted them all, standing with Coby at her back. "Thank you for coming." The pale mother reached out her hand. After a firm shake with Agents Johansson and Craig, she smiled sadly at Chief Barnes.

"Hello," Barnes said gruffly.

"Good to see you, Bradley." Maria touched his arm. "I thought you were with your daughter and grandbabies?"

"I came as soon as I heard." Barnes squeezed her fingers. "I had to be here to help bring Dante home safe and sound."

The words of comfort broke through Maria's thin veneer of strength, and she gave a deep painful gasp. Coby guided her as she sank down on a chair and bowed her head to the table, knocking a pen to the floor.

"Where's Dante's bedroom?" Agent Craig asked. "Agent Johansson and myself will go over each section of the home, but I'd like to start there. Also, the point of entry for the kidnapper." He put on paper booties to cover his shoes, and handed them out to her, Barnes, and Stephan.

Riley slipped them on and crossed the living room to Dante's bedroom, explaining about the missing clothing—all new for school, and his favorite pajamas. "It seems like the person who took Dante wanted him to have a few of his favorite things. As if he cared about the boy."

Agent Craig nodded in agreement. "Possibly someone he knew, then."

No one answered. It was a rhetorical question.

"Maria and Coby gathered photos of Dante to put on posters and nail them around town," Riley said.

"That would be good. Give Maria a job." Stephan nodded with understanding. "I hope we find Dante tonight, but if we don't, then they can be put up in the morning."

"I'll let her know." Riley returned to the kitchen, where Maria leaned against Coby's chest as he caressed her back and murmured words of comfort. It was a sweet and caring scene.

Riley cleared her throat. Maria faced her with a wan smile. Her long auburn hair was loose to her waist. There were so many questions she didn't know where to begin.

"Thank you, Riley. I'm sorry about earlier and any confusion. It's just that I'm so used to covering up my past, that I've forgotten how to unlock the memories."

Coby stood from where he'd been kneeling. "What happens now?"

"The FBI is gathering evidence," Riley said. "They'll search inside and out, looking for footprints or other clues that will tie whoever kidnapped Dante to the crime."

"I thought it could be Gino, but it had to be Marco!" Maria said. "He's still ignoring me now. Like he's punishing me. I even tried to call Ricky. Same."

"We don't know anything for a fact. If Marco Esposito is on this island, we will find him. If he has Dante, then we will get him back." Riley spoke with calm assurance.

Coby went to the coffee pot and refilled his cup. "Look, sitting on my butt is making me crazy. What can we do?"

"I was talking with the FBI agents, and they said if you make posters of Dante, that would be a good help."

"Really?" Maria asked, getting to her feet. "I have a color printer for the menus at the restaurant. How many copies should I make? I'll do a hundred or more if they want."

Coby read the clock on the wall. "It's only quarter to eight and it won't be dark until after nine. We can go hang them up right now!"

Riley raised her hand. "Let me check with our agents in charge. They said in the morning. I know it's hard to wait."

"Someone could put them up around the ferry dock," Maria said, anxious to see more action.

"I'll go ask. Maria, maybe you should go to Coby's for the night, and get out of here?" What if Marco wasn't just a goon as Maria thought. How had he found her? How long had he known, if he did, about Dante?

"I'm not leaving," Maria said resolutely. "What if Dante comes home?"

Coby smacked his palm to his fist. "Nothing makes sense to me—why would this Marco dude take the boy? Why come here and pick up his belongings instead of leaving the moment he had him?"

Riley considered this. "Well, maybe so that Dante would feel comfortable with his favorite things. If it is your cousin, Maria, what are his demands?"

Instead of answering Maria asked, "Was Ricky on the ferry too? They are usually inseparable. Tweedledum and Tweedledummer."

Pulling her phone from her pocket, Riley shot off a text to Matthew to check the ferry manifest for Ricky Russo.

Maybe it would be smart to have an officer around Maria's home. She and Matthew could take turns, and Rosita too.

"Wait here." Riley returned to Dante's room. Barnes was in the backyard with Agent Craig, searching for more prints, perhaps, or more clues.

Stephan had turned the lights off and was using a blacklight to show prints.

Riley waited at the threshold, waiting until Stephan noticed her. "I'll need the fingerprints of everyone who was in the room that should have been," he said. "Maria, Dante, the boyfriend."

"All right. Me, Mom, and Kyra. My daughter babysits Dante sometimes. We've been over for dinner."

Stephan stood. "I have a fingerprint kit in the case by the front door. Do you mind doing that for me?"

"Not at all," Riley said. "Maria was wondering if she and Coby printed the posters that someone could put them up tonight?"

Stephan straightened with a scowl. "I understand that she wants to be busy. So long as she is available by phone or nearby, in case we have word from the kidnapper. Has there been any strange calls today?"

"Other than from Marco, no. Maria doesn't know how he found out that she lives here and has a boy, but two weeks ago she got a text message from Gino Ferraro saying he wanted his money, then this morning, Marco wanted a family meeting in Brooklyn. There's been bad blood since before her dad died last month. After she found out that Marco Esposito was here in Sandpiper Bay, she panicked and called them both but neither responded. She wants to stay here tonight in case Dante comes home, but the kidnapper would have to be really stupid to stick around, wouldn't he?"

"Why would her cousins take the kid?" Stephan asked, not answering her question.

"My thought is that they're playing hard ball," Riley said. "They know she'd inherited some money when her dad died, and claim it belongs to them. What if they came to collect?"

"It makes perfect sense," Stephan said, "but if it were true why wouldn't she hand over the loot and get her boy back?"

"Marco is no longer communicating with Maria."

"At this point anything is possible and should be taken seriously." Stephan straightened from a crouch where he'd shone the light along the baseboard trim. "I get how invested you are. We are too, and we will find Dante. Barnes and C.C. are out putting up surveillance cameras right now."

Riley nodded. "I'll go update Maria and Coby about the posters and being available as well as the cameras."

Her phone rang and she answered Matthew expecting that by now he'd have news about Ricky one way or the other. "Hey."

"Darren was walking around the lighthouse and thinks he found something," Matthew said.

Riley's body filled with adrenaline. "What did he find?"

"A blue sandal with half a strap. Boys size six."

CHAPTER SEVEN

Riley nodded at Stephan and pointed her chin toward the door. He understood the silent directive and followed her to the broken back door. She didn't want Maria or Coby to overhear this news. In a hushed voice, she told him about the sandal being found with a broken strap and that it was near the lighthouse.

Stephan kept his voice low too. "You'll have to go check it out without alarming Maria. Let C.C. and Barnes know. They might want to join you. On the other hand, I need those prints done so we can start the cross reference of what doesn't belong in his room."

"Wouldn't it be better for Chief Barnes to go and for me to stay behind?" Riley was a team player even though she was eager to leave.

"You've been working this case from the beginning while Barnes is considering an early retirement because of his health." Stephan shrugged his big shoulders. "Don't sell yourself short."

"Thanks. I'll let you know what they decide," Riley said. Stay, or go? Most importantly she hoped that the sandal led directly to Dante.

"The sandal may not be his," Stephan said, bringing her down to earth. "It's summer and this is your tourist season, right?"

"You're right." Riley turned away, walking toward the kitchen where Maria and Coby were sitting at the table with the laptop open, designing a poster with Dante's face and Maria's cell phone number. Riley didn't disturb them. She glanced out the back window but didn't see Barnes or Agent Craig.

Riley texted Matthew to send her a picture of the sandal. She removed the paper covers from her shoes and went out the front door. Trees were on the outer edge of the property, not blocking the house, which made it easier to survey the home. Also harder for anyone to sneak up to it.

She heard Barnes and Agent Craig in the attached garage and went inside.

"Hey, Chief. Just got a text from Matthew. Darren called him saying that he found a child's blue sandal near the lighthouse."

Agent Craig, who had been adjusting the screen on a five-by-seven tablet, lowered it to follow the conversation.

Barnes pulled his phone from his pocket and read his notifications. "Matt called but we were putting up the cameras. Riley, why don't you go collect the sandal and bring it to the station?"

"Happy to but Stephan said that he needs prints of everyone who was in the house. Mine are on file, but Kyra babysat so she might need to be printed. Mom. So do Maria and Coby." Riley turned to Agent Craig, with a question in her eyes. "Well, should I go or stay?"

Agent Craig scowled. "What is it? Are you unable to collect possible evidence?"

"I can, indeed. This is not my first rodeo, Agent Craig." It seemed he wasn't going to countermand Barnes or Stephan.

"I didn't mean to imply that you weren't fit for the job; just thought you might be gung-ho and racing at the bit."

"I am." She still felt like Agent Craig was judging her. She wouldn't crack under pressure, but she was anxious to go, hoping that the sandal led them closer to Dante. She didn't have time for his power plays.

Barnes cleared his throat. "You won't find a better police officer than this woman. She has courage and intelligence." He nodded at Riley. "You go. I'll handle things here."

Agent Craig eyed Barnes and adjusted a setting on the tablet. "That's fine by me, but I'm coming with you."

Riley glanced at Barnes, thanking him silently for his commendation. "We don't know for sure if it's Dante's sandal or belongs to another kid." She turned her gaze on Craig. "I hate to take you away from here if you're still needed. Matthew and I can handle this."

Her phone dinged at the same time Barnes's did and they both studied the picture.

"It looks about right," Barnes said. Riley nodded, a knot in the pit of her stomach. This was the same style sandal Dante had been wearing earlier today. Riley had seen him wear the sandals often.

"I'm coming," Agent Craig repeated. "And I want in on the information loop."

"Good luck you two," Barnes said. "And keep the peace."

"Of course." Riley glared at the arrogant FBI agent, then laid a hand on her boss's arm. "Maria and Coby don't know about the sandal and perhaps they shouldn't. They've been making posters with Dante's picture and a number to call. They need something proactive to do."

"Got it." Barnes accepted the tablet from Agent Craig. "I'll get the fingerprints. See if Susan and Kyra can come to the station as well."

"I'll call from the car." Riley looked at Agent Craig. "You ready?"

"Yep. Let's go."

Riley unlocked her SUV and slid behind the wheel. It was

five to eight, which only left them a little over an hour of daylight. The passing of every minute weighed on her.

"We're going to the Sandpiper Bay lighthouse," Riley told him. "Darren rents an apartment downstairs and he's the one who reported the sandal."

"You know Darren?"

"I do. He's a vet suffering from PTSD. Anxiety. He helped Rosita and Coby with the search parties today. He's a good man."

The agent didn't say anything to this. Riley used her Bluetooth to call Kyra. Her daughter answered on the first ring.

"Mom! Have you found Dante yet?"

"No, hon." Riley could feel the agent's gaze on her as she slipped into Mom mode rather than officer. "The FBI is here in Sandpiper Bay. I'm in the car right now with an agent."

Code for she was not alone and to behave herself.

"They're here? Nana," Kyra called, "The FBI's here!"

The agent rubbed his smooth-shaven chin.

Riley sighed. "I need for you to go to the station and give your prints." She remembered there was nobody there to take them. "Oh, geez. I need to call Rosita…Matthew is out at the lighthouse. She can do the prints for you."

"Nana too?"

Her mother had been inside Maria's house plenty of times for dinners or movie nights. "Yes, Nana too."

"I'm not going to Paris if Dante isn't found, Mom. I told my teacher and Lennie already."

"Kyra!" Riley had bent over backwards to make sure that Kyra had everything done for the last-minute invite and now was not the time for her daughter to bring this up.

"I'm not," Kyra repeated stubbornly.

"We will talk about this later, Kyra."

"I'm not going to change my mind, so you better find Dante

fast." Kyra's bravado was all a sham, as her daughter's voice shook.

"We will do everything in our power. Now, let Nana know what's going on. I have to go!"

She ended the call and glanced at Agent Craig. "You have kids?"

"No." His curt answer was a clear sign that it wasn't a topic he was interested in continuing.

Riley called Rosita next. "Rosita, it's Riley. Listen, do you mind going to the station for an hour or so? The FBI are here, and we need to get the people's prints who may have been in Dante's room. Kyra babysat, so, we need to cross her off as well."

"Not a problem. I'm on file already, and I've filled in to watch Dante occasionally too."

"Thank you. We will add that to the report."

"How's it going? I'm so worried for Dante that I've been scrubbing my floors and reorganizing my kitchen cupboards."

Riley exhaled, wishing she'd alerted Rosita that they weren't alone. "Fine, fine. Uh, I should go. Thank you."

"I'll go right now. Oh, should I pick them up from the cottage? It's a hike from your rental to the station."

"They've got their bicycles but thank you."

"Okay then. I'm off!"

Agent Craig stared out the window, but it was almost as if he was trying not to laugh. At them and their small but talented team at the station?

Riley didn't care for that but also remembered when she'd felt the same, a big shot coming from Phoenix to Sandpiper Bay.

She'd grown a lot in the last ten and a half months. So had Kyra, and Susan. They were happy here, making friends easily and being warmly welcomed. Her mom had recently forged a friendship with Wyatt, the ferry captain.

Thankfully, they arrived at the lighthouse before she had to talk to anyone else. Darren was standing there with Matthew who'd changed into his uniform. Steep stairs led down to the beach.

Her first week here she'd discovered a dead body. Her professionalism had proved her capabilities to the annoyance of the chief who didn't want to hire her, because of her undeserved reputation as a snitch.

Riley parked and opened the hatch for her evidence kit. She slid it out and she and the agent stood before the men.

"Matthew. Darren. Darren, this is Agent Craig with the FBI."

"I hope you didn't trample the evidence," the agent said.

Darren backed up, palms out at the rebuke.

Matthew's cheeks reddened. "We haven't touched anything, sir. The sandal is over by the hiking trail into the woods."

The opposite direction from the lighthouse. "It wasn't near the water?" Riley asked. She'd assumed that whoever had Dante had taken him off the island via the water. Riley cleared those thoughts. Just facts.

"No," Matthew answered.

Agent Craig took out his phone to record notes. "Show us."

They tromped across the gravel parking lot away from the bay. In the distance, boats bobbed on the glistening water. Skiers, jet skis, and powerboats. Sailboats. This was summer on the east coast and folks enjoyed every second. They came from Boston and Bar Harbor and farther north. The smell of fireworks warred with salty air.

A sign read HIKING TRAIL 1.5 miles. There was one going down to the beach across large boulder-style rocks and another going up, into the trees.

"Where does this go?" Agent Craig asked. "Does it eventually connect to the park?"

"Yes," Riley said.

"Here," Matthew walked faster and pointed to a blue sandal with a strap. The strap was broken and the toes of the rubber muddy, as if the wearer had dragged his feet.

Riley's stomach flipped as she imagined Dante being dragged by...someone.

Agent Craig knelt and studied the sandal, and the dirt around it. He looked up at Darren, then Matthew. "You didn't touch it?"

"No," Darren said.

"No," Matthew seconded.

Agent Craig snapped pictures of the gravel of the parking lot, and the big boulders leading down to the beach. The grass on the trail.

Finally, he was satisfied.

"What do you see?" the agent asked.

She sensed it was an important question and examined the sandal again.

"It's broken," Matthew said. "Dante must have been forced to walk really fast and," he glanced at Darren and withheld mentioning Marco or Gino, "the kidnapper must not have noticed when it was lost."

Agent Craig looked at Riley with a raised brow. She remembered the muddy footprints outside the Catalina home. The gravel here, and the grass on the trail from the park.

"Dante couldn't have gone far without his sandal, especially without anyone noticing," Riley said, recalling Kyra's younger days. She wouldn't have gone willingly with a stranger. She'd struggle. The footprints outside belonged to Dante's and his abductor.

"What are you thinking?" Agent Craig asked.

"We have the prints behind the house which belong to Dante and whoever took him. Also, the fact is that this sandal doesn't belong here," Riley said. "Darren, was it here earlier when you and your team searched?"

"I didn't have this section, but Rosita would have the list of who did," Darren said. "If it had been here, it would have been a flag for sure."

Agent Craig nodded.

Riley donned gloves and drew out the evidence bag. She carefully put the blue sandal inside then sealed it, using a black marker to label the time and date.

"We have the best technology possible at the station believe it or not," the agent replied. "We brought the kit from Portland."

"The one Stephan had at Maria's?" Riley pocketed the pen and grabbed her keys anxious to see what the tools could do.

"We have another on the chopper." Agent Craig rocked on his heels.

"Let's go." She nodded with a half-smile at Darren. "Thank you."

Darren gave them a two-finger salute and headed down the path to the parking lot. "Let me know? I'm happy to search again." He gestured toward the bay full of boats and people ready to party. "It's not like I'll be catching any sleep tonight."

"I will." Riley unlocked the SUV. "Take care."

Matthew hopped in his sedan. "See you guys there. Oh, Riley —Marco Esposito had bought two tickets, cash. But Ricky Russo used a debit card on the ferry yesterday for drinks. Proof they are both on the island."

"Really? That's very interesting." Riley explained to Agent Craig about Maria's cousins and how they weren't supposed to know where she lived—yet they were here, and Marco had tried to call. When Maria called back, they hadn't answered. "I think we know who has Dante—but where are they keeping him?"

How had the sandal gotten to the hiking trail where anybody could have seen it, and yet, they hadn't…was it an accident, or had it been placed there as a taunt?

Back at the police station, Agent Craig and Agent Jeff were able to lift a partial print from the broken strap. Due to the muddy condition of the strap, it was not possible to determine with any certainty a match.

CHAPTER EIGHT

Agent Craig shook his head, his eyes frozen on the useless print. "Dammit!" he snapped. "The rap sheets for Maria's cousins showcase petty crime. They wanted to talk with Maria, but now Dante is missing, and they no longer want to talk. Why? They are in control." He strolled around the small room like a tiger sniffing for fresh meat. He stopped in front of the partial fingerprint photo. "We don't even know if they are still on the island. Did they panic and ditch Dante? Where?"

"What do you want us to do?" Riley asked. "We can work all night if needed. Finding Dante is our only concern."

"Thanks for letting me know." Agent Craig didn't bother to hide his sarcasm. "Here's something you might do. Enter this partial print into the database so we'll be able to link it with other matches if we get lucky. We need something concrete." He ruffled his short hair. "Would be nice if it came with a name on it."

Barnes had arrived at the station while Riley and Agent Craig were with Darren and Matt. "I'm on it," the chief answered briskly. His shoulders were slumped, eyes watery. The room was silent, spirits down as they realized the partial print might not be enough.

Somehow it had gotten to be nine o'clock and Rosita was heading home. She'd return to the station by eight the next morning. "Rosita, did Kyra and my mom come in?"

"No. Sorry." Rosita gestured to the portable giant whiteboard. "While I waited for them, I worked on the list of volunteers for the search party—those who have been interviewed about Dante and those who haven't. This couple was acting kind of strange, Mary Jo and Hunter, and they were part of the grid near where you found the sandal."

"Strange how?" Agent Craig asked.

"Jumpy." Rosita shrugged. "Just…off."

"I'll need their phone numbers and address so I can interview them privately," the agent said.

"They are tourists, camping in Mackabee Park. Here for the holiday weekend," Rosita explained. "Hunter's cell number is on the list. Patricia Cabot was very knowledgeable so she might give you reliable information. Cy and Teena George were also helpful, but plan on being gone by Monday."

"Good work," Agent Craig commended.

Rosita waved goodnight to them all. Had Mary Jo and Hunter placed the sandal on the trail? Leaving it to Agent Craig to check them out, Riley turned her attention to the ferry captain who might know more than he thought.

She dialed Wyatt's number and he answered at once. "Wyatt, just a few quick questions. You had Ricky Russo and Marco Esposito on your ferry yesterday. Can you do us a big favor and let us know if or when they buy return tickets? It's important for this investigation."

"Neither man bought a return ticket for tonight. My last ride out is at midnight, so I will be looking for their names if they do. The main fireworks will go off at ten from the boatyard," Wyatt said. "Coby dropped off Dante's picture and I've been showing it to everyone. It's most unlikely that the kidnapper would bring the boy onboard but if he does, we will know."

"Thanks, Wyatt." Riley ended the call, nodding to the chief. "That means the cousins are probably still on the island—unless they rented a boat? I'll pull up a list of boat rentals on the island and cheap one-night hotels. We can start there."

"Let's split the task. I'll handle the local marinas and ask about their recent boat rentals," Matthew said. "You do the hotels."

Riley gave him a thumbs-up and sent a quick text to Kyra to make sure she was okay.

"Good." Barnes and Riley stared at the clock on the wall in the breakroom which seemed to be on hyper-speed. 9:30. 9:40. She sat before her laptop at the oval table and found six boutique hotels, not including private vacation rentals.

She struck out at the first three on the list.

Jeff checked in from the helo where he'd been doing surveillance of the island and the surrounding area. "The fireworks are about to start so we need to park this until later. What's the plan? Where do we want to put this baby to rest?"

"There's a hangar in Bangor, so head on over when you're ready," Agent Craig said. "I'll send you the coordinates."

"No need, my copilot Elizabeth has it on her screen. We can rest onboard and get a fresh start in the morning. Fuel up there. The sky is lit up like New Years out here! Incredible. Later, guys."

"Roger that. We'll be doing rotation shifts here at the station," Stephan said. "Night."

Riley stepped away to quietly answer her phone, Kyra's face on the screen. "What's up sweetheart? Figured you and Mom would have stopped by."

Kyra sniffed. "My bike had a flat tire. Just my luck. What do you want us to do?"

"Let me check. Rosita already left but maybe I can come pick you both up." Riley held the phone away from her face and directed her question about the fingerprints to Chief Barnes.

"Bring them in tomorrow morning. That'll be soon enough."

Riley gave the chief a grateful smile and relayed the information to her daughter. "It's been a long day, you two get some sleep. I'll pick you up in the morning or have Rosita swing by."

"I'm not sleeping through the firework show, Mom. Wait. You're not coming home?" she asked with surprise.

"Not yet. Maybe later," Riley said. "Love you!" She ended the call before her daughter could argue.

Matthew whooped and pumped a fist from his seat at the table, the laptop before him as was his phone. "Cool news."

"What's up? You're almost jumping out of your skin." Riley knew every expression on his face. "Let's hear it. Did you find a boat rental made to Marco or Ricky?"

His cheeks flamed. "Not about the case, sorry. Jeff offered to give me a ride on the helo at five when they come back from Bangor in the morning." Matt looked at Barnes, then Agent Craig.

Barnes rubbed his heavy brow. "Don't see why not—after you go home for a few hours to get some sleep."

Agent Craig snickered. "No reason to say no. Riley needs to rest as well. We all want to be sharp in the morning. Dante's life depends on it."

So did their reputation, Riley silently added. "Did you reach the marina, Matt?"

"No answer anywhere. Guess they're going out to watch the firework show," Matthew said. "I'll keep trying."

Barnes swiveled his seat around. "Just got a call. A man named Hank Grover from Bar Harbor said he and his family were at the park today and heard a boy's cry around two this afternoon. Found this kid's leather sandal. Thought it might be important so they picked it up and placed it along the track where it could be easily found. Said they didn't stay because his kids were hungry, and his wife didn't want to be involved. They returned to their original spot, packed up their belongings, and took a ferry home."

Riley pulled up Wyatt's roster for the day. He forwarded each one as it happened to keep her current. Sure enough, Hank Grover. Hannah Grover. Two kid tickets. Leaving the bay on the 3:00 p.m. ferry. "I've got confirmation."

Stephan, who had just walked in, heard most of the story. "So, you mean the sandal, our only physical evidence to a possible crime, has been contaminated. Just effing great!"

"Settle down, Stephan," Agent Craig snarled. "Get a grip for God's sake." The muscled blond amazon with blazing blue eyes appeared angry enough to do serious damage to anyone in his way.

Riley and Matthew got up in a hurry, backing away from the table to stay out of harm's way.

"We only could get a partial and it's in the database." The cool-as-ice agent moved right into Stephan's space, his nose almost touching the furious giant's chin.

Agent Craig had some balls, Riley had to admit. She and Matt exchanged alarmed glances. Barnes stayed at the table, watching the men.

"You under control yet?"

Stephan's face was almost purple. He flexed his muscles. "No, sir."

"You want to kick someone's ass, don't you?"

"Yes, sir. Starting with yours if you don't get out of my way."

The silence in the room was palpable. Riley was holding her breath and Matthew's face was tight with tension.

Barnes wore an amused expression. "That's enough, *boys*."

They both glared at the chief who returned his attention to a screen with the map of Mackabee Park.

Riley opened her mouth to say something, but Matthew pulled her forcibly back.

It took a few seconds until Stephan's mouth twitched. He put his fists up in a defensive response and then lowered them a second later. He snickered and glanced around. Suddenly he roared with laughter. Agent Craig joined in, and Riley grinned too when the two men bumped each other's shoulders.

Obviously, this had not been their first time blowing off steam.

Stephan flopped into one of the chairs, head down as he sucked in air.

Barnes stood up. "If you two could explain what that was all about, I'm sure we'd all like to hear."

Agent Craig answered, "This dumb ass has got it into his head that a crime such as this needs to be solved in six hours or less. His first case had not been successful and from then on, he set himself a personal goal. He hates to be wrong. Even by a few minutes."

To Riley's surprise she noticed the now gentle giant was wiping his eyes and staring at his feet. His shoulders were shaking, and she wanted to give him a hug. Common sense prevailed.

The sound of fireworks was audible through the building, and they all rushed out to watch the show. Riley regretted not being with Kyra and her mom, and she imagined what Maria must be going through right now.

Knowing that Dante was afraid of the fireworks and unable to comfort him.

After about thirty minutes the show was over, and they all trekked inside pausing by the front counter.

Barnes stopped at his desk and Riley noticed the red message light flashing on the landline. He pressed play. A frantic young male voice said that they'd had an incident with a crazy driver who'd smashed into their dingy and ruined it. The driver was fighting with a woman, probably his wife, and there was a little boy onboard, crying. Maybe because of the fireworks, but what if it was that boy people were looking for that got lost at the park? Our boat is sunk, the teen said, frantic, and someone should come rescue them and arrest that guy for boating under the influence. And crazy. By the giant anchor. The call abruptly ended.

The voice on the line had sounded like a teenager and drunk as a skunk.

"They're lucky they didn't drown," Riley said, "from too much alcohol."

Stephan checked his watch. "It's eleven now."

Matthew stood over the chief's shoulder, listening to the message again. Riley shifted close to Matt who made room for her.

Agent Craig cleared them away with his sinewy muscled arms held wide. "Can you get a hold of that kid?"

"They didn't leave names or a phone number, but I can try to reach them with the callback feature." Chief Barnes made a few attempts, but only reached the busy signal.

"We're on this." Matthew dipped his head toward his partner. "Riley and I will bring these kids to the station for questioning."

At C.C.'s nod, the two of them were out the door, tires spinning as they raced to the only location it could be. The giant anchor was made of iron and had been on the island for a hundred years. With luck the boys would still be there and confirm the first possible sighting of Dante. They were pumped but not to the extent that they ignored the search they'd been working on before this call.

As Matthew drove, Riley texted the marina that he'd contacted earlier, asking for them to call the Sandpiper Police Department. She left a number and shared that it was extremely important as it involved a missing child.

"Where is the Coast Guard through all this? Riley asked. "I

can't stop praying that this might be the lead we need to find Dante."

"Stranger things have happened."

"Most cases are solved by something right out of the blue. Just a tip, or something that triggers a memory which connects the dot." Riley's stomach churned. They passed the anchor, but the kids weren't there. "Matt. We can't go back without those teens. Where are they?"

"We won't. There's a small bay near here that they might have come ashore that isn't as rocky."

Riley glanced at Matt as he drove. "That was some crazy shit back there with Stephan and Craig. I guess they have to blow off steam somehow. Right?"

"Guess so. But if you ever freak out on me like that, I might need to file a complaint."

"Yeah. Totally fair."

The area was hemmed in by old oak trees and heavy moss, creating a frightening image in the darkness. The teens must be terrified. Riley knew her daughter would be—then again, Kyra had enough sense not to put herself in that position.

When Matthew pulled up to the bay, they spotted the three teenagers right away. Seated on a long log of pine, looking wasted and forlorn. Riley said a silent prayer that her only beloved daughter was safe and home with her Nana—a guardian angel for sure.

Nightingales were fluttering amongst the heavy oak trees, birds tweeted back and forth as they skipped from limb to limb, and she distinctively recognized the *peck peck peck* of a woodpecker hammering on a tree as if to compete with the occasional fireworks. Running water from the creek nearby and the scent of the woods filled her nostrils as she and Matthew stepped out of his sedan.

The boys stood, appearing delighted that the Calvary

arrived. Matthew kept his flashlight lowered so he wouldn't blind them.

Riley gave them with a friendly smile. "Hi, bet you're happy to see us, aren't you?"

They nodded their heads and shuffled their feet. "I'm Officer Harper and this is Officer Sniders. We're glad you reached out to us. We'll get you home safely, but we need to take a detour first."

"I'm Sam Tyler," the tallest blond said. He nudged the redhaired youth to his right. "This is Shane, my brother."

"I'm Charley," the brown-haired kid said. He hooked a thumb over his shoulder to the pieces of boat bobbing in the bay. "And that is the remains of the dingy that douchebag ran over."

The older teens were both dressed in jeans and T-shirts with emblems on the front and Boston Red Sox Caps. Shane had knee-length cargo shorts and a white Celtic tee.

Matthew stepped in. "Bet you guys are hungry after a long night."

"Damn straight! We can't wait to get off this island," Charley said. "Some creep ran over our dingy. We shouted when we saw his big fancy boat coming toward us, but he didn't even slow down."

"Good thing you weren't in it. Or you'd be toast." Matthew gave a friendly grin.

"We had to jump overboard!" Sam said.

"You must be the one who made the call, is that right?" Riley asked.

"Yes," Sam said with a shrug. "So?"

"We need you guys to come to the police station and file a complaint. After that we would appreciate your help by answering a few questions that might help us solve a crime. Cool, right?" Matthew scuffed his boot to the ground.

"Sure, I guess so." Sam and Shane exchanged a look. "Didn't you ask if we were hungry?"

"No worries, we've got you covered," Matt assured them. "There's pizza."

"How old are you boys anyway?" Riley asked, leading them to the car. "Do we need to notify your parents?"

"My cell phone worked so I already called." Sam Tyler seemed to be in charge, so she'd concentrate on him.

"I'll need that number to inform the FBI," she told them.

"The FBI? That's cool."

Riley hid a smile. Hadn't been long since she'd thought it was cool too.

Sam rattled off the phone number and his parents' names, James and Sherry Tyler. Riley sent the information by text, so the parents wouldn't be worried and could find them.

"I'm eighteen," Sam said, "and my brother Shane is sixteen. Charley will turn eighteen next month." Sam took off his hat and stuffed it in his back pocket. "My mom and dad were on the way to get us but now they gotta wait for the next ferry."

"No boat, no ferry, lucky you got a call through to us." Matthew opened the back door for the young men. "You've got nothing to be afraid of, except for one huge FBI agent."

"You're kidding us, aren't you?" Shane's eyes rounded in fright. Of the three he was the one who was still obviously under the influence.

"Nope. Just show some respect and answer the questions and we'll keep him chained up." Riley shot an amused glance at Matthew.

During the short ride to the station, the teens talked non-stop.

Charley said he saw a boy too but didn't get a good look. "Might have been a girl, cuz I couldn't see the face under the hat."

"Thass right," Shane piped up. "They had the music blaring. But the dude was fighting with his wife. That much I know."

"Thanks guys. We appreciate your help," Riley said.

"So," Sam glanced at the others and smirked. "If we help you find this creep who practically ran over us do we get to be on TV or what?"

Matthew looked at the boys in the rear-view mirror but kept quiet.

"What happened? Did that jerk face in his fancy yacht grab that kid? No wonder he was in a hurry!" Shane's voice squeaked as he was elbowed by his brother.

"That's what we need to figure out." Riley turned her head. "If you boys can help find Dante, the missing child, I'll make damn sure you get your hour of fame."

Matt winked at her. They were as always on the same page. Making the kids comfortable, possibly heroes, could set this investigation in motion. They couldn't make Stephan's six-hour window but perhaps they'd have Dante back in the morning. Riley'd take that as a win.

On their arrival the boys ducked as they saw a helo above the sedan with whirling blades dropping from the sky. Mathew rushed them inside. The teens were wide-eyed with excitement and Shane whooped with glee.

"Forget TV," Sam told them, gaze still glued to the chopper. "I'll take a ride in that and call it a deal."

Matthew laughed. "Wait your turn, kid. I'm next."

~

BARNES, IN HIS OFFICE, STOOD TO WELCOME THE YOUNG MEN, AS did Agent Craig. Stephan pushed up from his too-small chair and eyed the boys. Shane let out a yelp and hid behind Riley, who grinned at all three.

"Better sit down, Stephan," Riley teased. "Don't wanna frighten the kids."

"What did you tell them about me?" the agent groused.

"The truth, nothing but the truth. I'm asking you to behave, okay?" Riley sent a warning smile…these were impressionable young adults. Stephan needed to show constraint.

"Let's take this to the breakroom, shall we?" Agent Craig had his hands on the older boys' shoulders as he led them down the hall to the large table. Barnes followed closely with a trembling Shane by his side. Stephan made sure to take a seat at the far end from the teens but close enough to make eye contact.

Riley and Matt stood behind the young men for moral support.

Agent Craig tilted his head and rubbed his dark hair. "We have a surprise for you, boys. Someone you all know is climbing out of that chopper right this minute. Any idea who?"

Sam jumped out of his seat. "The bad guy or…or--"

His parents burst through the back door into the kitchen and Mrs. Tyler sobbed as she gathered her sons in her arms. The father joined in the hug, including Charley in the family circle.

"Mom, Dad, how did you find us?"

"Captain Barnes and Agent Craig heard we were stuck in Bangor and had the crew fly us in." Mr. Tyler reached out his hand and shook both of theirs, then introduced himself as James and his wife as Sherry.

Stephen knocked over his chair as he lumbered over to the family. "I'm Agent Johansson, pleased to meet you."

Charley's eyes grew wide as he stared at the giant next to him. Stephan put a light hand on the boy's head, bent and whispered in his ear.

Riley couldn't hear what he said but Charley grinned and high-fived him.

C.C. and Barnes had rustled up some food while they were

away. Leftover pizza, pretzels, and a pan of steaming lasagna that Matthew's mother Martha had brought over. She'd included two loaves of garlic bread already sliced on an angle, and a case of beer.

"You!" Stephan gave Matt an angry look. "Were you keeping that amazing woman away from us? Saying bad things?"

All eyes were upon Matthew. C.C. shook his head and told Stephan to sit down and stop being an ass.

Matthew's face matched his red hair. "No, no! Of course not. This is my mother we're talking about. Admit it. You all can be a little intimidating."

"Huh. Martha didn't think so. Matter of fact, she promised us food for as long as we're here. I think she's crushing on me." Stephan snatched two slices of the garlic bread and slid his chair near the table.

The boys sat across from him and kept their gazes on the bubbling golden-brown lasagna, their tummies rumbling from hunger.

"Ah, hell." Stephan got up and cut three large wedges from the untouched lasagna pan. "Here you go," he placed the food in front of the boys. "You all need it more than me."

The parents had already had dinner, so they accepted two beers and allowed the interrogation to begin.

CHAPTER NINE

Once the lasagna was consumed and the table cleared, Riley watched Agent Johansson use his considerable charm to put the teens and the parents at ease. He talked about boats and reckless drivers as if having a boat rammed into the rocks was an ordinary occurrence.

Not true, but that didn't seem to matter by the end of the interview. The boys had seen one person, male, average-size and wearing a cap, behind the wheel. The woman he was arguing with had been a strawberry blonde. The little boy or girl, possibly around Dante's age. Maybe? They couldn't agree on how to identify the child even when shown Dante's picture.

"We would like you to take a look at this photo," said Agent Craig. "If you don't recognize him that's fine; we'll move on."

The three teens passed around the mugshot of Marco Esposito. "Could this be the possible driver?" They all said no.

Riley was disappointed, as were the others. Fact was that Marco was dark, like Dante, and the driver had a slim build with light-brown hair. After Matthew pulled up some photos of different sizes and types of boats, the boys were able to identify one that looked the most like the boat in question. A forty-two-foot power boat with red trim, and a name on the side.

"I think it started with a C," Charley said.

"One word, or more?" Stephan asked patiently.

"Not a C," the younger boy said.

"Like you'd know," Sam scoffed.

"I was puking over the side, so I got a closer look," Shane countered.

His father, James, popped him lightly on the back of the head. "Serves you right for drinking."

"I'll never drink again," Shane swore.

Stephan's mouth twitched. "Not a C?"

"No. It looked like a D to me. D for dick," Sam snorted.

His mother corrected him. "Be serious, Sam. Not a smartass."

"Sorry." Sam squeezed his eyes closed as if that might bring the memory into the now. "Hold on. I think it was a G. And a girly name, a short one."

"Gina?" Agent Craig asked. "Gino?"

"Maybe, I'm not sure, sir."

"Pretty Girl," Shane jumped out of his seat. "That's it for sure."

Barnes frowned. "Pretty Girl? That puts us back to zero," he muttered.

"You're sure?" Stephan asked. Riley was impressed with his composure, especially considering his previous outburst regarding the sandal and the fingerprint.

"Yup. I'd bet my turtle on it."

His mom and dad laughed. "He loves that thing. Calls it Sunday, as that was the day he captured it." James winked at his boy, a spitting image of himself.

During the end of the interview, Barnes answered a call from Hank Grover. The chief asked if Hank's prints would be on file. The man must have said no, because he agreed to go to his local station on Sunday to give his fingerprints. Riley felt like there were more questions than answers.

"Okay. I think we have enough for one day." Agent Craig stood and thanked the boys. "You did well. Your parents must be proud." He shook hands with Sherry, then James. "Okay if I call you, if we need to?"

"Of course," James said. The clock on the wall read 11:30.

"The last ferry is at midnight." Sherry expressed concern. "We should hurry."

"We'll have an officer drive you to the depot," Stephan replied. "Thanks again for your assistance."

Agent Craig had been listening in while adding his own notes. The station phone rang, and Riley picked up. "Sandpiper Bay Police Station."

"Riley? It's Coby."

"Hi." Riley walked with the phone down the hall toward her office for privacy. "How's it going? How's Maria?"

"She's exhausted. I convinced her to at least doze for a while in her room. Barnes cleared us to use the house again."

"Good that she's sleeping."

"Anything new?" Coby's voice was strained.

"No, I'm sorry." Riley opened her office door. "It was smart to drop off the posters of Dante with Wyatt—he's been handing them out and is on the alert. You might want to get some shuteye yourself."

"I can't. I promised Maria I'd stand guard while she slept," Coby said. "I've been texting with Jessica all night. The Piazza Pizza staff are also very concerned about Dante."

Riley recalled the way Jessica had watched Coby earlier that day at the park, and wondered if Coby was aware of the crush she had on him.

Not that it mattered. It was obvious how much he loved Maria. "I'll keep you in the loop with what I can. Did you oversee the cleanup of the kiosk at the park?"

"Nah—the Piazza crew handled it." Coby sighed. "Jessica said that tonight's fireworks were the best ever, but what would she know? She told us this was her first summer on the island."

"Maybe she'd visited with her family?"

"Jessica might have mentioned it, but I wasn't really listening. She can be a chatterbox sometimes."

Riley chuckled. It was true but she attributed the chattiness to Jessica's youth.

Coby continued, "We saw a little of the fireworks from Maria's lawn, but we weren't really into them. All Maria kept saying was about how Dante is afraid of them. Who would do this?"

"We will find whoever is responsible." Riley didn't go into detail of the partying teens and the sunken boat. The reckless, probably rich *and* entitled, boat driver who had put the kids in harm's way. The possible sighting of Dante. "Will the restaurant open tomorrow?"

"Maria has asked the staff to open from noon until seven. This is a big tourist weekend, and it's important to fill the coffers for winter. I've got Tommy watching the bar at my place, so the Shack's in good hands. I've asked Jessica, Rob, and Parker to be on standby, though."

"A good idea." Riley read her watch. Quarter till midnight. "Has her cousin tried to contact her?"

"Not a freaking peep. She's asked me to read her phone for notifications. This is just so cruel."

"I understand. It's hard on all of us but way worse for the mother."

"I gotta go," Coby said abruptly. "I hear Maria stirring. Riley, this is killing her—please find Dante. She's terrified and I've never seen this woman afraid."

"Did she tell you any more about Gino? Or the family business?"

"Not a word," Coby said, sounding hurt at being excluded.

"I'm sorry," Riley said for the hundredth time today.

"I knew she had secrets, but they didn't matter," Coby said. "Just because I'm an open book with a tendency to overshare doesn't mean everybody is. Her secrets made her mysterious. Now, I wish I'd pressed."

The couple had been quietly seeing one another for the past few years, but Maria had been careful because of Dante. *She* was Dante's mother, and it made a little more sense now as to why she'd wanted to keep people from getting too close.

Coby ended the call with a quick goodbye, and Riley was left to stare at the phone. Relationships were messy and she'd opted to not have anything serious. Katie at the Lobster Pot had a very cute brother who had shown an interest, but it hadn't gone anywhere because Riley had been a very slow mover.

The Tylers herded the young adults before them toward the front door, passing Riley standing on the threshold of her open office.

Various mumbled apologies from the boys followed shy smiles as they exited into the parking lot. Sherry turned to Riley with thanks. "It's unbelievable to think they could have died tonight. Will you catch the jerk behind the wheel?"

"We will do our best," Riley said. "Pleasure cruisers don't have to be registered with the Coast Guard. All you need is a certificate to operate a boat. Our marina here at Sandpiper Bay has certain rules if you're going to moor in the harbor. I'll be checking to see who has registered at the dock, but with all the traffic this weekend, it might be a challenge."

Sherry's cheeks reddened with anger. "That's not right."

"No," Riley agreed.

"I'm just happy our boys were able to swim to shore," Sherry said. "Swimming lessons from the time they were three years old."

James nodded at Riley. "Good luck with your search for that little boy. We'll hug our kids a little closer tonight."

Matthew scooted around Riley to the front door.

"What a nightmare today has been," Sherry said. "Our boys safe, but one child still missing."

"Dante will be found," Riley said. "Your kids have been a great help."

"Thanks." Sherry waved and she and James joined their teens outside.

"Matthew, be sure to check with Wyatt since you'll be at the depot?"

"Yup. See you in a few." Matthew left and Riley locked the station door behind him. Almost midnight. She was so wired there was no way she could rest. Where was Dante? Who had him?

She returned to the breakroom and began calling the hotels to see if two single men by the name of Russo or Esposito had checked in.

Agent Craig sat next to her with a cup of steaming coffee he'd microwaved. "You should get some sleep. Tired officers make mistakes."

"I'm not tired." Riley was pumped on adrenaline.

"You have a hard time following directions or is it just me?" the FBI agent asked in his chilly way.

"Nothing personal, sir. That sounded like more of a suggestion," Riley said. "I've never been much of a napper."

Chief Barnes snickered and got up from the table. He glanced again at the maps of the park he'd laid out. Stretching his back, he watched Riley dialing another number. "If you're not leaving, should I make another pot?"

"I'd go for a cup," Stephan said with a yawn. "Those teens got lucky tonight." He stood and strode to the whiteboard. "If it was Dante on the boat, that's good news. Means he's alive."

"And if he's not with Marco Esposito then who has him?" Riley snapped her fingers. "We should have showed them the picture of Ricky!"

"Except that Ricky is dark like Marco," Agent Craig said.

He had a point. Riley felt Agent Craig's gaze on her as she reached yet another answering machine on her hotel search. Her phone rang. Matthew.

"Hey! Any news?"

"Wyatt does not have Ricky Russo or Marco Esposito on the ferry. The Tylers are on board, and impressed with our station," Matthew informed her. "I'm on my way."

"See you soon." Riley hung up and turned to Agent Craig, dialing number nine on her list of hotels.

"What do you hope to accomplish?" the agent asked.

"Maria's cousins arrived yesterday. They were not on the ferry home. So where are they?" Riley ran her hands through her hair and sighed. "They're still on the island." She gave the agent a stern look. "They are here to get the fortune they believe was left to Maria. Yet, no attempts to find it. What is their ultimate plan? I know they are up to no good, so we need to be sharp."

His tablet dinged an alarm and the agent jumped up to answer. Stephan and Barnes were one step behind facing the camera. The surveillance cameras installed at Maria's home had a direct link to the station. A single shadowy figure crossed Maria's yard, then disappeared out of sight.

"Who was that?" Agent Craig asked. "A cousin?"

Riley shook her head. "No. Not big enough. My guess is Jessica. She works for Maria at the restaurant, Piazza Pizza."

"Why is she sneaking around her boss's yard?" Stephan asked.

"Could be because Jessica has a crush on Coby," Riley suggested.

"I say we go find out." Agent Craig checked his pockets for keys only to remember that he'd come in the chopper.

Seemed fate wanted them with Maria right now. "I'll drive," Riley offered.

Barnes looked from Agent Craig to Riley and bestowed a sage nod. "We'll hold down the fort."

Nice, Riley thought with amusement. The chief was all about tossing them together. Didn't he realize that she excelled in focusing on the job no matter who she partnered with?

She got in the SUV and started the engine. "Sirens, or no?" This let Craig know that even though she was driving he called the shots.

"We don't want to wake the neighborhood." The agent buckled up.

"Who knows? It might be her or someone else dropping off some flowers. We need to keep our expectations low. Less disappointing."

"I would agree with that assessment." The agent glanced at Riley. "You know the back road to Maria's place?"

"Yes." Seven minutes later, Riley rolled to a stop beneath an oak tree that shielded their vehicle from Maria's front yard. The occasional fireworks from a nearby island brightened the sky.

Agent Craig held out his tablet. "This Jessica person came to the back porch, and then something spooked her. She left fast. Let's see what she was doing."

"Okay." Riley turned off the car.

"Do you know where Jessica lives?"

"No. Maria might. It could be on her employment form."

"Good. Quiet now." He held a finger to his lips. The FBI agent didn't make a noise as they crossed the street to the front gate. His stealth approach made her glad he was one of the good guys.

They stepped soundlessly around the side of the house to the back door. Coby and Maria stood at the window, looking out to the yard. Coby had his arm around Maria as she wore a stoic expression.

Still quiet as a whisper, Agent Craig pointed out footprints beneath the window. A woman's size seven or so, about her own size. The broken back door had been repaired, the knob shiny and new. Coby's handiwork?

Was Jessica involved with the kidnapper? A shiver ran over her skin. Had Dante walked hand in hand with Jessica into the woods then back to the house?

What fell short for her was the reason. Jessica and Maria were both from New York. Was that the connection? Could Jessica be in league with Maria's cousins somehow?

Riley motioned with her head to Maria and mouthed, "Should we knock?"

Agent Craig scowled but finally nodded. He led the way to the front entrance and allowed himself to make normal sounds as they scuffed along the path.

"We should ask about Jessica's connections to New York, maybe," Riley suggested. "She could know the family."

"Good thinking."

"I've noticed the way Jessica watches Coby, with stars in her eyes," Riley whispered. "And when a young woman looks at a cute guy that way, it means only one thing. She wants him." What if it had been more, like getting close enough to Maria to help the cousins?

"Maria is terrified," Agent Craig pointed out. "That was clear on her face just now. You sure Coby and Jessica aren't messing around?"

A person could never be one hundred percent.

Maria answered the front door with a rush of wind. "Yes?" She sagged to the frame. "Riley, thank God it's you. I've been seeing shadows all night."

"Not shadows," Agent Craig said, bringing out his tablet to show Maria. "Do you know who this is?"

Maria studied the image with surprise. "Jessica?"

"Yes. May we come in? We have some questions for you," Riley said.

"Come on back to the kitchen," Maria said. "I can make coffee or tea if you prefer."

The landline in the hall rang and Maria jumped. Coby appeared from the living room. They all glanced at one another.

"Hello?" Maria paled. "Chief Barnes. What are you saying?" She shook her head and handed the phone to Riley in disbelief. "Someone broke into Piazza Pizza!"

CHAPTER TEN

Riley put the phone on Speaker. "Chief, what's going on? Are you at the restaurant right now?"

"Yes. You two need to get over here to Piazza's."

"But how..." She walked toward the sofa, lowering the volume. Agent Craig stayed close enough to hear every word.

"Matthew realized that we hadn't checked Maria's place of business though we had cameras at her house. Great instincts." Barnes sounded like a proud father. "Anyway, he drove by and around to the back of the property and noticed a door cracked open. He called me immediately and waited for backup. We entered together but whoever broke in was already gone."

Could Jessica have been at the restaurant before coming to Maria's house?

Agent Craig commandeered the phone. "Don't contaminate the area. Have Stephan bring his tools to dust the scene for evidence. Let's hope the perp made a mistake we can use to find Dante. We will be there ASAP."

"We're coming with you," Maria said. "It's *my* business."

After an exhale, Riley nodded. "Come on then. I'll drive." She followed Agent Craig out the door.

Maria attempted to lock up, but her shoulders were shaking, hands fumbling with the keys. Coby took them out of her hands, locked it firmly and slung his arm over Maria's shoulder in support. Hard to believe that he'd mess around with anyone else, Riley thought.

"Be sure to ask about Jessica while we're in the car. I'll watch their faces while you're behind the wheel," C.C. murmured quietly.

Riley tipped her head in consent. Facial tics often gave away clues, whether a poker game or an investigation which could include a life-or-death decision.

She started the SUV, turned while the vehicle was still in park, and smiled at Coby, sitting behind Agent Craig, and Maria behind Riley. "Hang in there, guys. We're getting closer to finding Dante, but we have a few questions."

Maria was mopping her face with tissues and sniffling, so Coby answered for her. "Of course."

"Maria, have you heard from your cousin, Marco? Or Ricky?"

"Not since this morning when Marco was blowing up my phone about a family meeting. I called back and it's gone to voice mail. Same for Ricky. My own cousins ghosting me. I almost called Gino, although he's the scariest man I know, but I'd do anything if it would help me find Dante, that's how desperate I am."

Riley and Agent Craig exchanged a quick glance. "Did you call him, Gino?" she asked gently.

"No." Maria's face turned pink as she gazed at the man she loved and trusted, then sat up straighter to gain control over her emotions. Riley empathized with her friend who'd had a traumatic day, her world swiftly shifting.

Riley arched a brow at Agent Craig. His long legs were cramped in the front seat as he shifted to keep his gaze on Maria. He gave her a slight nod.

Riley began the short drive from Maria's home to the restaurant. What did Maria know regarding the friendship between Coby and Jessica? She needed to tread lightly and not create more doubt. The Coby that she knew was a man in love and honest to a fault. Or was he?

As gently as a police officer and friend could she said, "Maria. Someone broke into your restaurant. Dante's missing. I don't believe in coincidences. Could this be a mob target against you?" Calling Gino would be inviting the fox into the hen house.

"It must be connected," Maria admitted. "But why would "they" take my son?"

Agent Craig cocked his head as he shot her a "what the hell" look. Riley lifted her chin and kept her voice firm but friendly. Her patient approach had worked before, but the situation had escalated. No more secrets. The truth, the whole truth, and nothing but the truth.

"Maria, answer carefully. No more lies or hedging."

"I'm not! I've been honest with you. More than with anyone else in my life."

"Okay then. Have you noticed any suspicious behavior or someone taking an interest in you, Coby, or Dante in the past few days?" Riley thought of the list on Maria's table. "Even someone you consider a friend who might be acting different?" She had an opportunity to show Agent Craig that she had a handle on this and didn't want to blow it.

Maria's hot breath from behind Riley scalded with her angry exhale. "I have built a life here on the island and I'm very careful with who I allow close to my son—like your daughter. Even then, he was still kidnapped."

Riley winced at that dig—but it told her they were getting closer to a truth Maria wanted buried.

"A warning?" Maria's shoulders slumped once more, and Riley hated to pressure this woman who'd only shown kindness to her and her family. Her life was spinning out of control and shattering the belief that she had made a haven for herself and her son.

But she must. Dante's life was in the balance.

"Taking your son is more than just a warning," Agent Craig said in a detached tone. "It's a felony and the abductor will be punished with prison."

Coby nodded. "Damn straight."

"It seems that we've gone full circle back to the cousins," Riley countered. "They are on the island and have both opportunity and incentive."

"What incentive?" Agent Craig growled. At her or Maria?

Maria spoke quickly, not allowing Riley to answer. Another secret? "They wouldn't do anything without Uncle Alphonso's approval. I told you, they're goons."

Riley eased off the gas, wanting more answers. Piazza Pizza was just around the bend. "Do you know why Jessica might be hanging out around your house this late at night?"

"No. She's so young though," Maria said. "Maybe she wanted to console me but then saw Coby? She reminds me of myself when I arrived on the island from New York. A lost soul. Before the miscarriage."

"Is Jessica from your area in New York?" Riley drove so slowly it was practically a roll.

"I'm from Brooklyn, she's from the Bronx." Maria sounded like she pitied Jessica.

Agent Craig shifted on the seat. "Jessica was sneaking around your property and didn't make her presence known. We need to learn everything we can about her. Where she came from, her background, who she knows on this island. Is it possible she knows your family in Brooklyn? Might she be in contact with them? Any detail you can think of no matter how small could be important."

Maria sucked in a deep breath and released it slowly. Tears

were still streaming down her cheeks but at least she was no longer sobbing. "She's been working here for two months and is a good employee. Friendly with everyone, happy to work extra hours. She's a summer hire and I was thinking I'd offer her a full-time position, she's that sweet. I don't believe that she's out to con me."

"Jessica is not a suspect," Riley said softly, responding to Maria's defense of her employee, "only a person of interest."

"Isn't that the same thing?" Coby's voice held an edge. "She fills in for me sometimes at the bar if we're shorthanded."

Riley hadn't known that. Jessica was enmeshed in both Coby and Maria's lives. "How was Jessica's relationship with Dante?" Riley met Coby's eyes, then turned her attention to the road. They were in the parking lot of the pizzeria. "Did she socialize with anyone? Like, a boyfriend?" Riley parked next to Matthew's sedan and the chief's SUV but kept the engine on and the doors locked.

Maria held Coby's gaze and nudged his arm.

Coby cleared his throat. "Look...she is a young, spirited woman and has flirted with me on several occasions. I let her know that I'm in a relationship with Maria and intend to stay that way."

"When and where did the last "flirtation" take place?" Agent Craig asked, watching Maria. Riley realized that Maria had known of the crush since Coby was open about it.

"Friday, day before yesterday. Jessica was filling in for a waitress who was out sick."

"Where do you work, Coby?" the agent asked.

"I *own* a bar called The Shack—if you want to check it out. We had regular hours today and don't close until two." His chin was firm, his tone wary as he answered the FBI agent.

Agent Craig gave a little snort. "Not necessary—at least for now. Do you think Jessica working with you could be tied to Dante's abduction?"

Riley glanced at Coby. His nostrils flared with anger. "It's not."

Riley inwardly acknowledged that everyone was on a tightrope without a net. "Cool down, Coby." She released a long breath. "Let's start over. Maria, can you tell me Jessica's full name please."

"Jessica Bianchi. Nineteen years old. Her parents immigrated from Sicily in nineteen-ninety-five with their eight-year-old daughter. Jessica is the second child." Maria patted Coby's knee. "No records, but obviously bright as she attended NYU with good grades. She left before graduating when her dad had a stroke. I can actually give you her social security number from the employee file if we can get out of this damn car and go inside."

Fair, Riley thought. She turned off the engine and released the door locks.

"Hmm," Agent Craig said slowly, not getting out and holding them hostage with his unrelenting gaze. "Let's dig deeper and see what's on the other side. Why would she be here, isolated from the rest of her family doing a waitress job? No offense Maria, but her resume seems a little fabricated."

"I hate that you're making me doubt my decisions." Maria balled the tissue in her hand.

"Does Jessica have a key to the restaurant?" Riley asked.

"No. Everyone has a code on the alarm," Maria said. "Before you ask—everyone who is an employee knows it!"

"And the alarm didn't go off," Riley said.

"No." Maria bowed her head. "Which means it's someone we know. Maybe they just forgot to shut the door and there will be a rational explanation."

Coby spilled from the SUV first. Maria slid out next. Riley joined Agent Craig by the open door. She could hear Matthew and Barnes inside. "Keep your hands to yourselves," he told Maria and Coby. "That means no contact with anything until we know the place has been thoroughly dusted. Don't touch a wall or a doorknob—nothing."

Barnes skipped the greetings and waved them forward. His face was ruddy and sweat rolled down his face. Riley was reminded of his ill health and wondered if he should be running this operation. Not that she could stop him. There was something genetic in a good officer's makeup that meant protect and serve despite the personal consequences.

They walked through the hall to the restaurant and bar. The kitchen was in the rear and orders were slid through a vast opening. In the dark, even the gorgeous murals Maria had painted looked eerie.

"What did you find?" Agent Craig asked Barnes in a low voice from the office threshold. Stephan was shining his flashlight around an open wall safe. Riley made out the shadows of a desk and overturned chair, file cabinets. Computer. Not a random theft but they were after something specific.

"See for yourselves." Barnes studied each face and Riley knew he trusted them all when he continued, "The safe is empty. Done in an orderly fashion like they were pros. Meaning the lock wasn't broken so they had skills, or knew the code."

Riley glanced at Matthew, who nodded. The Brooklyn cousins were petty-crime professionals.

"Me and Coby are the only ones who know the safe combo." Maria, forgetting about Agent Craig's orders not to touch a thing, switched on an under-the-counter kitchen light then let out a scream. Graffiti covered three of her beautiful walls.

Few people knew of her artistic talents, but she'd painted scenes from the Amalfi Coast, the Roman Coliseum, and the Trevi Fountain. They brought her joy.

Coby wrapped her in his arms and whispered, "We'll redo the walls, and it will be as wonderful as before."

Maria clung to him like a lifeline which right now he probably was.

Riley swallowed a taste of envy seeing the love they shared. She'd had boyfriends in college and a lousy husband but nothing as sweet and strong as this.

"What did I just tell you?" Agent Craig threw his hands in the air and pointed at Barnes. "Make a mental note that switch was touched by Maria *after* the break-in."

Barnes typed the note into his phone. "Done." He tapped his temple. "Cell is much more reliable than this these days."

"Sorry," Maria whispered.

Stephan was in conversation with Agent Craig. Riley stepped closer to try and overhear the conversation. The money was gone. The boy taken. If they couldn't find the key to the mafia money, this might've been the cousins getaway cash, their means to return to Brooklyn.

Matthew crossed his arms ensuring that his hands were clearly in sight and not touching anything as they waited for Agent Craig's go-ahead. Or Barnes'. Someone above their pay level.

Barnes studied Riley and Matt, correctly interpreting their frustration. "Why don't you two search outside?"

Riley felt like they were being told to go play and let the big kids get the work done. She shook off the sentiment, accepting that this was also important.

"Sure," Riley said. "Nothing better to do."

"Don't get sassy, Officer Harper." Barnes held back a smile.

As they passed the office, she heard Stephan say that they'd finished dusting the area around Maria's safe. Barnes had found two sets of footprints instead of one. Agent Craig headed for Maria with a glint in his determined eye.

Maria and Coby were huddled together in the hall until Agent Craig separated Maria from Coby. "If you want the FBI's assistance, you have to be honest. Tell me about the Russos in Brooklyn?" His question was pointed, as if he believed she withheld important information.

"I can't," Maria said, lifting her chin in the air.

Riley wanted to shake the woman. Didn't she realize she might be impeding efforts to save her son? What power did the family have over her?

Barnes noticed them standing in the open doorway. "Go. Do a thorough check outside," he instructed. Matthew grumbled but he and Riley exited the restaurant to canvas the surrounding area.

Riley nodded at Matthew. "You want the parking lot or the children's playground behind the restaurant?" Her gaze sharpened as she examined the parking lot. Police vehicles, trees on the perimeter. The street was normally quiet at this time of night, but the fireworks had folks up later than normal. "I don't care." She flicked strands of hair from her cheek.

"Okay. I'll take the lot then," Matthew said. He left immediately, using the flashlight on his iPhone to illuminate his path.

Tiny mosquitos flew around her as Riley wandered toward the side of the building and the small jungle gym Maria had installed so that Dante could play while worked. She swatted at the mosquitos that made her itch. Frogs croaked. The moon was covered by a cloud. She hoped that her mom and daughter were sound asleep. Were the footprints Barnes had found two different men? The idiot cousins? Better yet, would they lead to Dante, or was this a fool's errand and distracting them from Dante's kidnappers?

A loud shout echoed around the property and Riley ran toward her partner. Matthew waved Riley over, pointing at the ground. He withdrew an evidence bag from his pocket. "Have a look. I think we've found something."

"You mean *you* found something. Good work, Matt." They bumped shoulders and bent lower to see the glowing cigar butt and a trampled area under a large fir tree. Riley got goose bumps and her nape tingled but when she searched the shadows, she didn't see anyone. Not Jessica or Marco. Nobody.

"It's too hot to put in the bag," Matthew said.

"The person smoking this cigar was just here," Riley surmised. "Why don't you go tell the others while I stand guard?"

Jubilant, Matthew hurried off and returned almost immediately with Barnes, Stephan, and Agent Craig. The cigar butt still glowed, meaning the culprit could still be here watching them, possibly annoyed by their near capture.

Coby had his hand on Maria's waist as they stood in the parking lot. "What did you find?" Maria attempted to escape Coby's hold, needing to see for herself.

"Just a cigar," Riley said loudly to calm Maria down. Most likely she'd thought the worst… that it was her son lying in the dirt, no sign of life. Riley reached the couple and one look at Maria's stricken face confirmed it.

Riley took her by the shoulders and peered into her eyes. "It's not him. Maria, it's only a cigar butt. It might help us find the person who took your son so we can deliver him home. Have faith and think of this as happy news."

Coby whistled through his nose. He appeared to be holding on by a thread. They all were. Riley spoke in a concise manner, "This is about as intense as it can get, but each clue, small as they seem, brings Dante closer."

Chief Barnes joined Riley to speak with Maria and Coby. With a few minutes to spare before the FBI ripped into Maria's story, Barnes gave her a warning. "Maria, I know you worship your boy. I also know you want Dante home safe and sound, just as we all do. But I need to ask…are you hiding any information from us that could hinder the case?"

Maria pulled away and stormed off toward her restaurant without answering the question that hung in the air.

Coby cursed. "None of this makes any sense. The motive here could only be to frighten Maria, right? What do they want from her?"

"We don't know," Riley stepped forward. "Maria's reluctance to speak about these cousins of hers, who just so happened to show up the day before her son goes missing, is highly suspicious. If it were me, I'd be throwing them under a bus in order to ensure the FBI's cooperation. We know they've done jail time and yet she hasn't spoken badly about either one. It's alarming."

"I agree." Coby glanced toward the restaurant where Maria had disappeared. "Every time I start asking about them, Maria freezes up. If they have Dante, what is she waiting for?"

"I can't answer that, but I'm sure that the FBI will get the truth out of her," Riley said.

The two wily agents had noticed that Maria was alone and broke off their conversation with Matt to follow her into Piazza Pizza. Barnes had also left their circle and after a quick squeeze to Coby's hand, Riley raced off to catch up with the others.

She put a hand under his arm. "How are you feeling, Chief?"

"Could be better," Barnes said softly. "This is one of our own. I've known Dante since he was a tot."

This case was personal to Riley as well. "It's good to see you in action. Now, let's put our great minds together and find these thugs."

Coby stood where they left him, looking so forlorn that she waved him forward. The three of them entered together, finding a table next to the agents who were already grilling Maria. They were in a corner of the dining area and her head was down, long lush waves hiding her face as her shoulders drooped.

Coby leaned over and whispered into Barnes ear, "Maria wouldn't put Dante's life in danger—I know she'd step in front of a train to keep him safe."

"Yup," the chief said. "I agree. Let's see what she has to say."

"Ms. Catalina, for one last time." Agent Craig had his scary face on. "Tell us about your involvement with your cousins and make it quick before we charge you with hindering an investigation!" His voice thundered through the empty restaurant.

Even Riley jumped.

Maria's head jerked up and she half stood, her hands on the table for support. "I don't want to talk to you," she said with defiance and stared toward Riley. "I'll tell Riley."

Riley moved across the restaurant to peer into her friend's eyes. "It's too late for one-on-one, Maria. Focus on me but understand that everyone in the room wants to find Dante. Think about your son." What hadn't Maria shared earlier?

In a quivering voice, Maria whispered, "It could have something to do with the stolen money."

Riley drew in a discreet breath and gestured for Maria to proceed. Stolen money?

CHAPTER ELEVEN

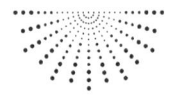

Riley didn't take her gaze off Maria as the woman darted glances around the room. She peered at Coby, then Barnes, but not at the FBI agents.

"My father laundered money for the mob."

Coby gasped. The agents were quiet behind Riley. She wondered if they already knew this, and that it was motive for the kidnapping. Had they kept their own secrets from the Sandpiper Bay police department? If so, it rankled.

"How did that come about?" Although Riley had known this, Coby hadn't. Was their relationship strong enough to survive?

Maria bowed her head. "For years Dad must have been skimming a little each month. I had no idea about the money he'd been stashing away, and to be honest, I never thought he'd have the cojones. I mean, the mafia? That would be like signing your own death warrant. Maybe when he got sick, he thought it was his chance to provide a legacy. The theft wasn't noticed until after he died last month."

Clearing her throat, Maria kept her eyes on Riley who nodded for her to continue.

"Gino Ferraro is the money collector for several pizzerias in

Brooklyn under mob control. He's got a brutal reputation as an enforcer. If you don't pay, there are consequences." Maria gulped and twirled a ring on her forefinger. "My uncle and cousins took over the business when my dad wasn't able, well… they should have noticed before this but didn't. Made them look bad."

"How much was stolen?" Riley spoke softly, afraid to spook Maria further.

"Millions." Maria stared down at the table, her shoulders trembling. "I inherited that money when Dad died. I don't want it." She looked up at Riley with truth blazing from her eyes. "I never wanted that dirty money. My cousins tracked me down when I was at the lawyer's office to discuss my *inheritance*."

"What happened?" Riley believed Maria was finally coming clean.

"The lawyer had a black eye. I knew he'd been…compromised. It's amazing how effective violence can be to coerce someone to your will," Maria said in a low tone. "I was raised with that violence and learned how to avoid it. Mom sometimes forgot and Dad would remind her." She punched her fist into her open palm.

"How long did you know that your father was laundering money?" Riley asked.

"It was never mentioned or alluded to. Still, I knew that we were living beyond our means, like having the biggest house on the block. It wasn't a big deal. Dad wasn't buying flashy cars or anything." Maria lowered her lashes.

"The name of your lawyer?" Agent Craig asked.

Maria didn't look at him but jutted her lower lip, focusing on her silver thumb ring.

"It will be a matter of public record," Riley said softly. "We need to know everything, Maria."

"Tomas Fielding," Maria said at last.

"What happened when you arrived at his office?" Stephan's tone was designed to make the bad guys shake.

"I noticed his black eye first thing," Maria blurted. "I was sure that anything I said wouldn't be in confidence. I knew my cousins had been there. Marco smokes these awful cigars, and the room still had that stink to it."

Riley nodded, making a mental note to see if the cigar from outside would match any prints of Marco Esposito.

"Mr. Fielding said my dad had changed his will after I was there several years ago," Maria said, swallowing hard.

Riley wanted to offer the desperate woman a glass of water but was afraid to break this string of truths. Was she thinking of Gino's attack in the chapel after she'd visited her father's sickbed? Had she even been honest about that?

Maria flicked her tongue over her dry lips.

"Did you expect to inherit anything?" Riley asked.

"No. Not really. Maybe a few things from my mom, perhaps a little of his own money, not the laundered stuff. At Dad's bedside I told him about Mom putting money away for me, hoping I could start a new life." Maria looked up and steepled her hands together in prayer. "I can see her smiling down at me right now, because I did. With her start-up money I had enough to open Piazza Pizza which has done very well for me and Dante." Her eyes flooded and her voice choked. "Dante, where are you? I'd give everything I own to have him back in my arms again."

"Your inheritance?" Agent Craig prodded.

Coby got up to fetch Maria some water and she bravely carried on after a sip. "I wanted my dad to know that I was financially secure without his help." She shrugged. "It really hurt my heart for him to be so sickly, but I didn't want any of his money."

"Did you tell him at any time that you lived on Sandpiper Bay?" Barnes asked in a comforting voice.

"God no!" Maria shook her head. "Dad thought I lived in Oregon on a tree farm."

"Tree farm?" Coby asked.

Maria focused on the glass. "Not a job that could be useful to my family in any fashion." Like money laundering.

Riley realized how deep the cover story had gone and how well Maria had kept herself safe from prying eyes. Until recently.

"Dad had originally left everything to his brother, and my cousins. He changed it so that his shares of the pizza parlor went to my uncle, and I received the cash. Not that I have it—it's in a bank vault in Brooklyn," Maria said. "There's a safe deposit box that I haven't opened."

"Why not?" Riley asked. She'd be curious if their roles were reversed.

"It's got my mother's wedding ring," Maria said with a sniffle, "and a letter, Mr. Fielding said. As much as I wanted to read that letter and have her ring, I couldn't. You know when you get that creepy feeling that you're being watched? That's how it was with me."

"Couldn't you have asked for protection when you entered the bank and asked to be taken to your vault?" Agent Craig asked.

He was the voice of reason, and that earned a chuckle from Stephan.

"I panicked, okay?" Maria held the glass of water tightly. "Maybe I'm not as cold and professional as you guys, but I had a son at home and wanted to be sure that nothing happened to him or me. I went right to the airport."

"Maria! How frightening! You should have told me." Coby didn't need permission from the FBI; he was there to support Maria. Riley admired his steadfastness as he waited for her to finish the water. "Were you staying at your dad's house?"

"No. A hotel. Under a fictious name." Maria looked over the

empty glass at Riley. "I refuse to go back to Brooklyn. I can live without knowing what's in the box."

"Don't be rash, Maria. Your interest in the box might bring back Dante," Riley informed her.

"That's true." Matthew scrubbed a hand over his tired face. "Your dad wanted you to have that money, but he didn't think it through. Good intentions. Bad reasoning."

"How many others know that you're a recipient of this alleged stolen money? Do we need to add more names to our ever-growing list of suspects?" Agent Craig shouted. "Holding a child or family member hostage is a well-known mafia tactic."

It was obvious to everyone present that he wasn't buying Maria's version of events.

Maria bristled. "At my father's funeral, Uncle Alphonso cornered me in the church. Said that something was wrong with the numbers, and he wanted me to make things right, before we both ended up floating in the river."

Riley and Matthew exchanged troubled glances.

"Exactly!" Agent Craig said.

"Cousin Ricky was on one side, and Marco the other." Maria shuddered. "I just wanted to go home but I had the appointment with the lawyer the next day. Mr. Feilding had stressed the importance that I see him before I left for Oregon."

Maria had done a good job with her cover story, yet she'd been discovered on the island within the month of her return from the funeral. Had her cousins followed her?

"Didn't you have any allies?" Coby asked. His words conveyed concern for Maria, not disrespect.

Maria pushed aside the cup. "No. I thought the lawyer might be on my side, but when I showed up and saw his black eye, I knew better."

"Do your cousins work for the mob directly?" Matthew asked.

"Not sure. I think their only connection is through the

percentage paid to the mob of money laundered through the pizza parlor. Gino collects the money. He's the kingpin and the cousins are the lackies. Before I caught my flight home Marco texted me. Said Gino was putting the pressure on about the missing money, and someone was going to pay." Maria touched her throat. "Possibly with their life."

"Not unusual," Barnes commented, rubbing the side of his nose as he did when stressed.

Riley could feel the FBI agents humming with questions for Maria but to her surprise they held back.

"I told Marco to keep the damn money." Maria lifted her head and stared at the FBI team in a moment of defiance.

"Maria, don't you think it's possible that your cousins have your son?" Riley asked. It made sense to her, but also alarmed her. What would the cousins do if threatened by Gino, the enforcer?

"Of course, I do! I'm still praying for a better explanation." Maria sobbed. "I don't have the money here with me and they know I don't want it. I made that clear." She made a mewing sound and tears spilled over. "Don't you think I would have given it to save my son? Why haven't they contacted me, if that's the case?"

"That's a damn good question," Barnes said. "What was in your safe here at the restaurant?"

"A few thousand for the month's expenses. I don't have a lot, but I have enough. It's all I wanted." She swiped the tears from her lashes. "Personal records like our socials and birth certificates."

"Tell us again what happened at the funeral?" Agent Craig inserted.

Maria stilled but eventually elaborated. "The family, maybe fifty or so people, were there to honor my father's death. My aunt stayed with my Grandmother Russo. My uncle was furious that my dad had backstabbed him and wanted me to make it right. I told him I didn't have Dad's money so I couldn't just hand it over. Problem was, I didn't know about the bank vault at the time. So now he thinks I'm lying."

"So, your family believes you *refuse* to give them the money?" Stephan asked, his voice rising with every syllable.

"Yes." Maria sighed. "Hell, they could go with me to get it. All they need to do is ask and give me my son back!"

Marco had tried to contact her that morning—so, what had changed? Why were they now offering radio silence?

Maria glanced at the FBI agents. "I don't care about the damn money. I would give it all to them for Dante! I know the family can be dangerous but thought I was safe. They had no idea that I had a son, so I thought he was safe too."

Riley peered across the room at Barnes. Laundered money, stolen money. "How did they find you after all this time?"

"I was being so careful, I told them I lived in Portland, Oregon. When anybody asks, I say I'm from upstate, never Brooklyn." Maria said. "I never say the Russo name."

Agent Craig stood and pointed to Maria's purse she'd brought with her. "Is that the bag you had at the funeral?"

"Yes," Maria said. "I used to change purses all the time, but since having Dante, this is big enough to hold everything."

"May I inspect it?" Agent Craig asked.

"Sure. I have no secrets," Maria said sharply.

With an arched brow at the statement, Agent Craig dumped the contents of the bag onto the table before them. A wallet, lipstick, and a brush. Hand sanitizer.

An Apple AirTag. He pointed to it as he pulled out a small evidence bag from his pocket. "This yours?"

Maria's eyes widened. "No."

"Considering what you've told us, it's probably how your cousins, or someone in your family, located you with this tracking device," the agent said, sitting back. "And now they've come to collect the debt they feel your father owed them."

Pieces of the puzzle were beginning to come together.

"Can we see family photos?" Riley asked. The teenagers from earlier had claimed that the man driving the boat that hit their dingy had light-brown hair.

"I want to go home." Maria stood. "I don't have any pictures. Not even of my mother."

∽

RILEY AND AGENT CRAIG HAD DROPPED OFF MARIA AND COBY AT her house just as the pink tendrils of dawn became visible by the lighthouse. The sky was lovely, but Riley was too bone-weary to give it more than a glance.

White sails from boats bobbed in the harbor, packed due to the holiday weekend. Today would be another day full of festivities completely at odds with the tragic kidnapping. She needed to talk with the folks at the marina about a reckless driver, possible damage to an expensive boat, and ask to see their surveillance tape. It was a long shot, but that's what this job entailed. Following trails that sometimes didn't go anywhere.

Matthew continued checking the boat rental places. How else would the cousins escape with a kidnapped kid whose poster was pasted all over the island? They had to be on the run, but she still believed they wouldn't harm Dante.

She followed the road away from the water, the image of a shivering and scared Dante overtaking her thoughts. Where was that poor child?

"You did a good job on that interview," Agent Craig said. "Maria trusts you and opened up with only you. You asked the right questions."

Riley half-smiled at him. "Only because you scared the shit out of her when you smacked the table."

"Teamwork." The agent shrugged. "I can see that there's more to you than the gossip suggested."

"Slander?" Riley countered, too tired to be polite about it. "I was blacklisted."

He rubbed his chin. "You did the right thing in Phoenix. I don't know if I'd have the guts to do that, but I'd like to think I would. You just *did*."

Riley acknowledged his words with a quick glance. "My family and I paid a heavy price."

"Would you do it again?"

"Yes," Riley said without hesitation. "The department in Phoenix has new management and I've received their formal letter of regret along with a job offer."

"Kudos." He chuckled softly. "You're a credit to law enforcement, and I'm sorry if I was a hard ass. Call me C.C.?"

"Sure." This was surreal. Riley parked at the front of the station as the helo was in the back lot. The rotor was visible above the single-story flat roof.

"You happy on this island?" C.C. asked.

"Mostly." Riley turned the engine off and blinked because her eyes hurt like they were filled with sand. She exited the SUV before C.C. could ask anything else. The apology felt great, but she didn't need a new friend.

Barnes was inside his office, head down on his desk as he grabbed a catnap. Matthew had run home to shower and catch two hours of sleep before starting all over again. The ride in the chopper would have to wait for another time. C.C. and Riley were on guard in case either of the suspects showed up. Not that they expected them to walk in and confess everything, but the officers' presence was important.

Still so much digging to do. They had yet to question the locals or engage those with watercraft willing to hunt the bay for an expensive large boat. Might be damaged or hiding out of sight. Not to approach said vehicle, only report it to the Sandpiper Bay police.

When Matthew returned, it would be Riley's turn to get

some rest. Agent Elizabeth was at Maria's place now, having arrived with the helo around five in the morning. The cousins were sure to make a move and every member of this team would be ready to nab them.

Riley didn't want to leave the office until Dante was found. It seemed like the ticking of each second put the little boy farther away. Most successful child recovery happened within forty-eight hours…seventeen had passed already.

"It's not reasonable to stay awake," C.C. told her as they closed the front door behind them. Was he reading her mind?

"Then why don't you sleep?" Riley countered.

"I will." C.C. ushered her down the hall to the breakroom. To her joy, the smell of fresh coffee greeted her.

Jeff was pouring himself a cup, bright-eyed and wild-haired. "Snatched two hours on the chopper. Highly recommend a nap."

"I'll go when Matthew gets here," Riley promised. "Did we get anywhere on the cigar butt?" She poured the fresh coffee into a large mug and took her first sip, then sighed with pleasure.

"Its brand is Montecristo," Jeff said. "Nothing more just yet."

"Could you get a print of some kind?" Riley pressed.

"Perhaps." Jeff sipped his coffee, in the caffeine zone.

"You can't talk to Jeff until after his first cup," C.C. explained. "Then he's all yours." The FBI agent chuckled. "Benefit of being with the same team for years. We know each other's quirks."

Which reminded Riley of what had happened yesterday with Agent Stephan. "Where is Stephan?"

"Catching some zees on the chopper," Jeff explained. "The chairs fold out and it's nice and dark."

"Want to try it out?" C.C. asked.

"No. I'll go home to my bed. I need to see my mom and daughter for just a minute and count my blessings. They are the reason I want the world to be a better place." Riley blamed the lowering of her guard on her exhaustion.

"It's a damn good reason," Jeff said. "I have two kids of my own and that keeps me going even when it's hard." He lifted his cup and pointed to C.C. "This man here lost a younger brother when he was a kid. Kidnapped by a stranger. Never found."

C.C. walked away from Riley, giving Jeff the stink eye. "Don't share my personal stories."

"Why not? We both did." Jeff shrugged, not affected by C.C.'s reaction. "It's not a secret. We all have something to motivate us. Carson was yours."

Riley went to the counter by the coffee pot and found a day-old muffin. It tasted fine but couldn't cover the bad taste in her mouth. What would she do if she lost her only child? Could she go on in this profession? Her gut said no.

"It's overwhelming all the bad around us—not just crimes but natural disasters." She glanced at C.C. who was studying the maps on the whiteboard. "How did we come to this?" Not waiting for an answer, she added, "I try to find one thing each day that's good and makes me happy. Like coffee and family." She raised her mug. How had C.C. coped as a kid? Losing his brother in such a terrifying way.

Taking her seat once again, Riley drank her coffee then opened her laptop and typed in some notes.

"Should we put the Apple AirTag on the whiteboard?" Riley suggested. She filled Jeff in on how someone, probably the cousins, had found Maria. C.C. quickly added the information.

"Smart," Jeff said. "Looks like we found our kidnappers. And yet they still run free."

"If they have Dante, which we believe they do—why haven't they contacted Maria? For a ransom, or exchange?" C.C. asked.

"Unusual for that not to happen," Jeff said. "Unless Maria's in on it."

"Sometimes the most obvious answer *isn't* the right one." Riley didn't believe Maria had anything to do with the money or her son's kidnapping. "We need to question Jessica today and find out why she was hanging around Maria's back door last night."

C.C. added that to the To Do side of the board, under call the marina, and check in with the guy about the sandal. Hank Grover.

"Cut the marina part." Riley told him. "I'll go there before heading home. I want to see the surveillance camera on Saturday afternoon. I'm curious whether a large boat limped in for repairs—seems like destroying a dingy would have created some damage."

"Matthew's working on that. You need your rest more than examining the docks for a damaged pleasure boat." C.C. left his To Do list intact.

Riley could see herself now, on hands and knees with a flashlight searching for a clue on each hull. The marina housed hundreds of boats. "If you insist. I have one last hotel to call, then I'll start on the vacation rentals."

"Sandpiper Hotel," a cheery morning person said.

"Hello!" Riley answered, surprised to reach anyone.

"Can I help you? If you're calling about a vacancy, we are full up," the voice said.

"This is Officer Harper from the Sandpiper Bay police station."

"Oh—is anything wrong?"

Uh. Now what? C.C. laughed at her from his position by the whiteboard.

"No. No. I'm just wondering if you have a guest under the name of Rick Russo."

"Hmm." The sound of coffee being sipped crossed the receiver.

"Or Marco Esposito."

"Now, I probably shouldn't be giving you any information without some form of identification. You may have to come down here."

"It's important," Riley said. "I can bring it by later, if it helps."

"Yes, please do." The sound of fingernails clicked on a keyboard and then she said, "Mr. Esposito checked in on Friday."

Riley's leaned forward, a runner at the starting line filled with adrenaline. "Was he alone?"

"What do you mean?"

"Did he have a child with him?"

"Fathers with their kids are the cutest, but I don't recall any children with him."

"Thank you." Riley typed a yes next to the name of the hotel. "Your name?"

"Susie. Oh, have to run—another call. Have a nice day!"

Jeff and C.C. joined her at the table, C.C. giving her a high five.

"I love to see hard work and persistence paying off," C.C. said.

"Let's go get them." Riley rose and patted her weapon. It was barely six in the morning, and they might still be asleep. "I'll feel better when those losers are in jail."

CHAPTER TWELVE

Tired as they both were, C.C.'s burst of energy matched Riley's as the agent's intense gaze rocketed from simmer to boil. "You want to make the arrest?"

"Hell, yes." Riley's bones ached, her limbs cried for rest, but those symptoms disappeared as she imagined rescuing Dante from the hotel and his captors. Besides, no way was she going to allow this cocky agent to steal her thunder.

C.C. chuckled as she glared at him. "Susie only identified Esposito. With any luck our friend Russo will be sharing the room."

"Lowlifes," Riley muttered, thinking of Dante. How would they subdue a child? Dante enjoyed video games and cartoons. She followed Agent Craig out the door and slid into the driver seat. Craig was used to riding shotgun since he'd been on the island. The sky was a soft grayish blue dotted with clouds.

"None of this adds up." C.C. glowered. "Why would they hang around a hotel room where they could be discovered? Why the lit cigar where we could find it? To taunt us? We might be on a wild goose chase that will lead us exactly nowhere. If so, they're smarter than Maria has given them credit for."

"Don't say that!" Riley adjusted her expectations of an immediate arrest and rescue. "The fact is the cousins are petty crime offenders. They aren't *killers*. Dante might be at the hotel right now." She glanced at C.C. "Ready to be used as a bargaining chip with Maria about the money. Maybe tied up or something? Shitty, yeah, but not deadly." Her nape tingled and she rubbed the back of her neck.

"Sounds logical. Let's hope you're right."

Riley stepped a little harder on the pedal, unconcerned about meeting somebody on the road. It was just after six and on this island the only ones up would be the roosters.

She pulled into the short driveway, flung the car door open, and hustled to the front steps of the Sandpiper Bay Hotel. Three stories tall. Landscaped with green hedges and white pebbles. Fragrant jasmine bushes. An American flag adorned the porch.

Agent Craig banged on the door, then finding it unlocked, they entered.

Feeling a little foolish about the banging part, Riley smiled as she greeted the young girl behind the front desk. She looked as though she'd just graduated from high school. Pink-cheeked, with bright blue eyes, and light brown hair in a swinging ponytail, she put down her novel on the counter. Her gaze paused at the name tag Riley wore on her Sandpiper Bay police uniform.

"Hello!"

What an awful job and dangerous too for such a young girl to work the night shift. Riley would never allow that to happen to Kyra.

"Susie?" Riley placed her badge on the counter as proof of her identity. "I'm Officer Harper and this is Special Agent Craig with the FBI. We spoke on the phone earlier?"

Susie's mouth gaped slightly, and she took a step back. "I thought it might be some kind of hoax, but you're real enough," she stammered. "Are you here for the men you questioned me about?"

C.C. opened his wallet, flashing his badge. "Yes. We think it's possible that you have two highly dangerous criminals staying in this hotel."

The poor girl recoiled, her skin blanched, and a look of terror flashed across her face.

Riley raised her hand to slow C.C. down. "Actually, Susie, could you verify if you booked a room to Ricky Russo?"

Susie logged onto the computer. "No...but Marco Esposito did ask for an extra key. Two queen beds."

"When is Mr. Esposito checking out?" Riley asked.

"He's booked for five days, so Wednesday." Susie scrunched her nose. "Do you mean that both of them are criminals? They've been very pleasant to me and are rarely around. They told me not to bother cleaning their room. I offered to drop off towels, but they didn't even want that." Her mouth trembled and her face paled. "Maybe I should call Mom. She's upstairs sleeping it off."

"Is that why you have the night shift?" Riley spoke gently. She'd make it a habit, if she stayed on the island, to drive by this hotel more often.

"I like it." Susie brushed off Riley's concern for danger. "It's usually quiet and I can get my homework done. I'm studying for my forensic pathology degree."

Agent Craig beamed. "A worthy career choice. Maybe you'll be working with us one day."

Susie blushed and tossed her ponytail. "As if!"

Riley got to the point. "What room are they in? I'd like a key in case they don't answer."

"Second floor, room 204." Susie lowered her voice. "What did they do?"

"Did you hear the news of a local boy going missing yesterday?"

"You think it was them?" Without waiting for a reply, Susie handed Riley the key to room 204.

"We don't know," Riley said. "As I'm sure you'll discover in your studies, policework is about asking questions."

"One answer at a time," C.C. agreed. "Thanks, Susie."

Riley found the stairs leading up and waved to Susie in the empty lobby. Had she ever been so young and innocent? Once at the second floor, Riley opened the door to the interior landing. Like most hotels, it was neutral in color, beige and white. The ice machine was to their immediate right, the long hall made of tile. "Two hundred." She pointed to the room across from them.

C.C. nodded and gestured that she should proceed. She listened sharply for anything out of the ordinary, very specifically, a child's cries. It was quiet except for the whirring ice machine.

Room 204. Riley knocked on the door. No answer. She and C.C. exchanged a look. The key meant they weren't exactly breaking into the hotel room but it was still dangerous because they had no idea what was on the other side. "High or low?"

C.C. grinned coldly. "High." He had his gun unholstered.

"Then I'll duck." Riley called out, "Maid service." No answer.

Damn. Riley hoped they were sleeping, and they'd catch the cousins unaware. She unlocked the door, ducking low as C.C. pushed it all the way open and entered the tiny foyer before the room widened to show two queen-sized beds, mattresses askew. Sheets and towels everywhere. Clothes strewn. No sign of Dante.

"Either they are really messy guests, or…"

"Someone's already been here." C.C. cursed loudly and inventively.

Riley put on a pair of rubber gloves from her pocket as did C.C. They picked their way through the mess that was left of the room.

Gritting his teeth, Agent Craig was seething as he dropped a men's sandy sock to the bathroom sink. "Dante's not here. I'm not sure he ever was. So, if the cousins had him, and this is still a big IF, why would they move without contacting Maria about the money?"

"I don't know." Riley felt like they'd lost momentum somewhere. She got down on her knee and searched under the two beds.

The room phone rang shrilly, and Riley got up so fast she banged her head. C.C. beat her to the phone. "Yeah. Shit. Thanks." He hung up and dragged Riley across the carpet to the closet. "Ricky Russo is coming up. Alone."

Her adrenaline pumped madly. She and C.C. barely fit in the tiny space of the closet but he cracked the door so they could see.

Ricky entered, not the least alarmed by the state of his hotel room. Dark hair, dark eyes, a pudgy physique that came from eating rich food. Loose cargo shorts. Was that a gun from his waist band? *When* had it been tossed? Was that why he'd stopped talking with Maria?

The goof ball didn't bother scanning the room to make sure it was empty—nope, he ducked into the bathroom to take a leak.

Riley widened her eyes at C.C. She held up three fingers. *On the count of three.*

One. Two. Three!

Riley strode from the closet, her gun trained on Ricky Russo as he flushed the toilet, C.C. at her back. He tried to grab his weapon but then raised his hands when he realized that there were two guns aimed at him.

"Who the hell are you?" Ricky demanded. His shorts sagged at his hips.

"Don't move," Agent Craig instructed. "You got a license for that gun?"

"No comment." His face grew splotchy like spilled tomato sauce.

Riley didn't want to waste time playing games. "Where is Dante Catalina?"

The cousin didn't flinch. The answer stunned Riley when he said, "Gino Ferraro has him."

C.C. kept his cool. "Gino Ferraro, Brooklyn mob? Money enforcer for a string of pizzerias in the City?"

"Yeah." Ricky shrugged and his pants slipped a little more. He wasn't wearing anything underneath. "We tried to set up a meeting with Maria, but she didn't answer. Then her kid goes missing and she's all over us. Serves her right if the brat gets it. Bet she won't try to screw over family again."

"Maria doesn't care about the money," Riley said. "Can you contact Gino? Get him to make a deal?"

Ricky's shorts fell all the way to his ankles. If he thought Riley would avert her gaze, he was wrong.

"Pull your pants up," C.C. instructed with a flick of his wrist.

That distraction was enough for the cousin. "Can't, asshole!" Ricky pushed her back into C.C. and all three sprawled on the floor—half in the bathroom, half in the foyer. Riley kicked Ricky's calf as he passed her by. In the several seconds that they were all tangled, the bastard escaped to the hall and slammed the door shut between them.

With a second gun Riley was unaware the mobster-wannabe had, Ricky shot the lock to trap them inside while he raced free.

"Holy hell!" C.C. shouted. "You okay, Harper?"

"I am. You?"

"Sorry about that. My fault completely," C.C. snarled.

Riley dialed the front desk and warned Susie to hide in the office, then hung up to use her cell phone to call the station.

"Barnes!" Riley placed him on Speaker so C.C. could hear too. "We just had a run-in with Ricky Russo. He told us that Gino Ferraro has Dante."

"Damn it! Come back to the station," Barnes instructed. "You both have got to be beat."

Her face heated at the fact they'd been bested by a goon. "Actually, Ricky broke the lock on the interior hotel door. We might need a different way out."

"Stuck?"

"Yes."

After Jeff and Stephan had a good laugh at their expense, the chief was too cool for that, the agents arrived twenty minutes later with a tool to take off door hinges for this sort of emergency.

She and C.C. had decided that the less details they shared with the others would be best.

As they entered the lobby to fill out a damage report that the police department would pay without question, Riley blinked, sure that she'd been seeing things. "Susie! Who is that girl?"

The lobby had a small café area for hotel guests with coffee and a continental breakfast.

C.C. stepped up to the desk. "Who? Oh. No way."

Susie's eyes grew big. "Jessica. She's been staying here the last two months at a discounted rate for cleaning hotel rooms on Mondays."

Riley glanced at C.C. This girl had to be the hardest working millennial she'd ever met.

"What do you think of her?" Riley asked in a casual way. She signed the form and dated it.

"Well…she's nice. Friendly. In fact," Susie giggled, "the day Marco and Ricky got here I heard them chatting with her, totally making idiots of themselves. Thought she was too smart for them but now I'm not so sure."

"Why is that?" Riley asked.

Susie lowered her voice to less than a whisper, "Ricky ran by me, in just a shirt! But he gave something to Jessica, I'm sure of it."

C.C. started to walk toward Jessica in the café, but Riley put her hand on his arm to stop him. She thought of their options.

Jeff and Stephan were examining the room the cousins had stayed in—she and C.C. could manage this and maybe fix their earlier mistake.

"Don't tell her I said anything!" Susie pleaded.

"We won't. Thank you, Susie." Riley gestured with her chin to the café. "Act natural, C.C. I could go for a coffee, how about you?" The long counter had a selection of coffee, teas, muffins, and cold cereal.

C.C. nodded. "That I could." They walked toward the cups as if they had all the time in the world. Jessica had her nose to her phone, earbuds in as she finished a muffin and coffee. Riley didn't see anything obvious that Ricky could have given her. Her tight-fitting tank top left no room to hide anything, but her short shorts had pockets. A hint of paper peeked from the side. The only other table in the café was occupied by an older couple with sunburns.

Riley filled her mug with Kona and circled the small area, the gun holster at her hip nose-level to Jessica. "Oh! Jessica? Hi!"

Jessica raised her head, startled to be called by name. "Hey," she replied cautiously, eyes on the holstered weapon Riley wore as part of her police uniform.

C.C. brought a steaming mug to Jessica's table. "Do you mind if we share?" He put the cup down, freeing his hands. His badge was attached to his belt.

The vein at Jessica's neck pulsed with alarm. "Sure?"

Ignoring the vacant chair to remain standing, C.C. said, "I'm Agent Craig with the FBI. We're here about the Dante Catalina case."

Jessica broke into a sweat and started to rise.

Riley shook her head. "Stay seated. We only have a few questions."

C.C. gave Jessica a chilling smile.

"Oh." Jessica perched on the edge of the chair. "Right. I feel really bad about Maria. Dante is her life."

She looked terrified, poor girl. Riley hoped she wasn't involved—either with the cousins or Coby for that matter.

"We'd like to ask about your friendship with Marco Esposito and Ricky Russo." C.C. tapped his badge. "This shouldn't take long."

"Of course, but I don't have much to tell you. Not really." Jessica wouldn't meet their eyes and stared at her muffin. "I only spoke with them for a little while around the pool."

"When was that?" Riley asked.

"Friday afternoon. I filled in at Coby's for a while for extra cash."

"And you didn't see them again?" C.C pressed.

Jessica sipped her coffee but choked from swallowing too fast. C.C. clapped her on the back—she scooted her chair from the table and the note from her pocket fell to the café floor.

Her face turned a painful red.

"What's this?" C.C. picked it up and offered it to Jessica in such a way that they could see the cash inside.

"Jessica…" Riley said with disappointment. Drug money?

Jessica held up her hands. "It's not mine."

Riley scoffed. "Jessica. I saw it fall from your pocket."

"We have agents upstairs." C.C. said. "With the ID kit. They can run the prints on this right now."

"That's right! Or we could go to the station," Riley suggested. "What do you think, Jessica?"

"Fine!" Jessica sank back to the chair so hard it sloshed her coffee. The sunburned couple in the corner had stopped chatting to listen. "It's from Ricky Russo."

"May we keep it?" C.C. asked.

Jessica flicked her fingers. "Go ahead."

"What's it for? Did you help kidnap Dante?" Riley's insides froze with anger at how Maria had defended this girl.

"No!" Jessica stood again as if her chair had a reject button. "I didn't. I did *not* have anything to do with that. This is payment for giving them the passcode to the pizza parlor."

Riley recalled the empty safe and missing money. "Why would you do that? Maria has always been kind to you."

Jessica glared at Riley. "Coby, obvi. I'm leaving tomorrow. I made a pass, and he turned me down. No reason for me to stay."

Coby had been honest with Maria about that. Riley pushed her coffee away. "We'll see about that. You need to come to the station for further questioning."

The sunburned woman said, "Shame on you!"

Jessica blushed and seemed sixteen instead of nineteen.

"Thanks for your honesty, Jessica." Riley patted the cuffs at her side. "Do we need to use these?"

"No. I'll come."

Susie's eyes widened with shock as she saw Riley escort Jessica from the café to the small lobby of the hotel.

"I'll be back to settle my bill," Jessica told her.

"We just want to finish asking you questions—that's all." Riley made sure to say it loud enough for Susie to hear. Innocent until proven guilty. What would be the consequence for giving the cousins the passcode and allowing them to steal and graffiti Piazza Pizza? Probation, a fine, or maybe a few years?

Agent Craig opened the door, and they went outside. Jessica shuffled her feet and climbed into the passenger side of the SUV. Once buckled in, she looked down at the floor. Her cheeks were red with embarrassment.

Riley got into the SUV and shut the air conditioner off before starting the engine. The sun was rising in pastel colors, and it would be another hot summer day, but she was chilled to her core. She waited for CC to buckle up in the back seat.

"Why were you at Maria's last night?" Riley asked as they drove to the station.

"You guys saw me?" Jessica buried her head in her hands. "I

felt bad for doing it. It was a stupid decision that I regretted but it was too late."

"We have cameras around to try and catch Dante's kidnappers. Did you ever see Dante with the cousins? Or meet a man named Gino Ferraro?" C.C. asked.

"Nope." Jessica sniffled. "Dante's such a cute kid. God, Maria and Coby are going to hate me now. Guess I don't have a job anymore."

C.C. gritted his teeth at her attitude. "Let's hope you don't end up in jail."

The remainder of the ride was quiet. Riley parked in front of the department, with Jeff and Stephan next to them in Barnes's SUV. They went inside and Riley put Jessica in Rosita's office to wait until they could interview her. They had holding cells in a separate building next door, but she hoped it wouldn't come to that.

Coffee. Riley needed coffee.

Barnes was on the phone in his office and Matthew hadn't come in yet. Jeff and Stephan were putting the prints from the hotel room into the database all via a computer in the breakroom. Riley went into her office, followed by C.C.

"The cousins don't have Dante. Gino Ferraro does. Why hasn't he made any demands on Maria?" Riley dropped her phone on her desk. "They must all be after the cash. Dante's only a tool, the lamb in all this. Do you believe Maria when she says she has no interest in the stolen money?" She did but hadn't gotten that sense from any of the FBI agents.

"I'm not sure. It's important that we're taking shifts guarding the Catalina house. Elizabeth will switch with Stephan in an hour."

Where are they keeping Dante? C.C. looked tired, irritable, and exhausted as he leaned against a wall next to the shelf with a picture of Riley with her family. The most important thing in her world. "This has been a strange case," he muttered, "we damn well need a break soon and it better start today."

Riley studied the agent who had lost all smug superiority and was now simply a man who wanted to save a child. Though it was just between them, it had been just a tiny bit gratifying to know that she'd held her ground when Ricky had dropped his drawers.

"C.C., I'm a hundred percent in agreement that this is a strange case."

Barnes knocked on the threshold of Riley's office door. "Nice work with Ricky Russo. We know now who has Dante which is worth any ding to your egos. That said, I'm ordering you both to get some rest."

Riley immediately started to protest, but the chief wouldn't hear it.

"You have ten minutes to wrap up a report and then I'm kicking you out. We can't find Dante if you two aren't at full speed." She'd never seen Bradley Barnes look so serious. And, just as she had with C.C.'s point, she agreed.

It was the fastest report she'd done in a while.

CHAPTER THIRTEEN

Riley pressed Send on the documents to Barnes and gave C.C., sitting opposite of her, a loopy smile.

"I hope Jessica is smart enough to cooperate with Chief Barnes," Riley said. "She's only nineteen and doesn't need to ruin her life, unless it's too late for that." She released a long breath. "What kind of trouble will she be in?"

"If she was working with Ricky and Marco of her own free will, it's more than likely she'll do jail time. Especially if we can prove she was involved with the abduction. That would be serious trouble. Unless, of course, she testifies against the cousins, but then she'll be watching over her shoulder for the rest of her life, waiting for the mob to find her. They don't take too well to informers."

Riley moaned, put her hands over her face, then massaged the back of her neck. "Can it really be that bad?"

"That's worst-case scenario, but if she cooperates, we can probably get her off on probation, no jail time."

Riley took a few sips of water from a ceramic mug. "Do you think Jessica knows where Ricky and Marco are hiding out? It's obvious that they won't be coming back to the Sandpiper Bay Hotel."

"Barnes will get all that information from her, and more. He's got good cop instincts; too bad he's in ill health. You taking over for him?"

"Haven't committed yet. Still have another six weeks on this contract but I'm concerned about my daughter and her lack of opportunities if we stay here."

"How does she feel about it?"

"Kyra has hinted she'd like to stay but that could always change on a dime, and Mom is hoping for another year. They've settled in after a rough start and made new friends. Mom is kinda dating Wyatt, the ferry captain. He seems really sweet on her, and it's been seven years since my dad passed away. She gets my blessing on this." Riley smiled softly and wiped away a tear.

Getting weepy meant she really did need to crash. As she stood and stretched her back, Barnes rounded the corner.

"You still here? Don't you ever listen?" The chief's face was bright red, and she feared for his rising blood pressure.

"Just leaving right now," Riley told him. "You doing okay?"

"Don't worry about me." Barnes jabbed his finger to his chest. "I'm too mean and stubborn to keel over."

"If you say so." Riley strode to the door, although that took some effort. "Call me if you need me."

"Out!" Barnes barked. "Now!"

Riley climbed into the SUV and drove the ten minutes home, her mom speaking with her to keep her awake the entire time. She told her that Kyra had fallen asleep on the couch while waiting for her. Like two peas in a pod, Kyra and her.

When Riley tumbled through the doorway, her mother took her arm and guided her to the kitchen, seeing how exhausted she was. Susan, always intuitive, handed her a mug of chamomile tea, an egg on toast, and watched her as she ate it all.

Seeing that Riley couldn't keep her eyes open any longer, Susan nudged her upstairs to her bed. "We already know the recent news, so go sleep. We'll talk later."

Riley didn't think she'd sleep but three hours passed in a heartbeat, and she was awake, feeling a jolt of adrenaline.

She shoved the comforter back, realizing she'd slept with her boots on.

Riley took the quickest shower in history, skipping her hair, and smoothing it in a bun. She raced downstairs where Kyra was at the kitchen counter, arguing with her mother.

"Hey!" Riley pressed a kiss to her teenager's bowed head. "What's wrong?"

"Nana wouldn't let me wake you up."

"Kinda glad about that. I feel amazingly refreshed after my long catnap. What else is the matter?"

"I'm not going on the trip," Kyra declared.

"You have to go. We've already paid, and no refunds. Lennie would really miss you." Kyra had been a last-minute addition thanks to her best friend's intervention.

"No. I won't go until Dante is found." Kyra's lower lip quivered but her eyes were dry. "It's my fault, Mom. I was watching him, and then he was gone."

Riley hugged her daughter to her. "Listen—you are not at fault. Now, you can't spread this around, all right? Maria doesn't know yet, so this stays here."

Susan and Kyra nodded.

"It has been a very busy morning, but...we know who has Dante."

"That's great!" Kyra said. "Why haven't you got him in jail?"

"We don't actually know where he is, just the name of the person who took him," Riley admitted. "We will have him back soon."

"That's wonderful news!" Susan said. "Is Dante all right?"

"We believe so. It's highly unlikely that this person of

interest would harm a hair on his head." Riley smiled with a confidence she hadn't felt since Kyra's SOS call.

"Coffee?" Susan asked Riley, handing her a steaming to-go mug with Sandpiper Bay Police Department on the side.

"God, yes," Riley said.

Susan placed a large cooler on the counter. "Sandwiches. Cookies. Tea. Make sure to eat, okay? I know how you get when you're working a case."

"Thanks. You're the best." Once again, Riley thanked her lucky stars for her thoughtful mother. "I've got to go, but Kyra, don't you cancel that trip, understood?"

"If you're sure Dante is okay and coming home, I won't do anything. I just couldn't be having fun while he's missing, Mom," Kyra said in a glum tone.

"We are going to find him, honey. Promise me that you will trust me about this and remember what I told you. You did nothing wrong."

Riley waited until Kyra nodded and then her upset teen ran to her bedroom. Torn, Riley wanted to go after her, but Susan handed her the cooler. "I'll sit with her. You go find Dante, which is the best cure for her blues. You've got this!"

"Thanks, Mom."

Riley, buoyed by positive vibes, was at the station at eleven on the nose. Nobody had so much as texted her an update and she was raring to get back to work.

The department was humming with activity when Riley entered. To her left, Barnes was in his office, examining large wall maps of the surrounding area. There were a lot of small islands off the coast where Gino could have easily stashed Dante.

For what purpose? There hadn't been any communication from him.

The receptionist didn't work over the weekend, so Rosita sat at Nancy's desk typing up notes as she juggled phone calls.

"Riley! I put the two tourists Matthew finished interviewing in your office. He thought you might want to speak with them. Hunter and Mary Jo. You should have a field day. Couple of stoners."

"I'll try to go easy." Riley's office door was cracked but she couldn't see inside from the lobby. "Where is Matt?"

"He's at the marina. Seems there was a sighting of Dante."

Riley gasped. "What?"

Rosita held up her hand. "Unfortunately, folks are "spotting" him all over the island. It's usually a false alarm. Almost always. They just want to help."

"What happened with Jessica?"

"During her interview with Barnes and Jeff, she swore that she didn't have anything to do with the kidnapping, only wanted to get her "revenge" on Maria by giving her cousins the passcode to the restaurant. Petty, stupid, and she is truly sorry." Rosita gave a little shrug. "She's been released and told to not leave town. A plus was that she'd overheard where the cousins *may* have moved when they switched hotels. A dive called the Drunken Pelican. She was warned not to contact them."

"Should I go check it out?"

"Nope. Elizabeth is going to do it when she comes back with Jeff."

"I see. C.C. and Stephan?"

"In the back. Well, Stephan is. Craig was forced out to sleep, just like you. How are you feeling?"

"Energized," Riley said honestly. "I'm ready to find Dante and bring him home."

"Maria's called a dozen times," Rosita said in a sad voice. "Hoping for updates. I wish I had something uplifting to tell her."

"I'll give her a call. Any progress on finding Gino?"

Distracted, Rosita read a note to her left. "I'm sure you'd be the first to know. Before C.C. left, he ordered a trace on Marco and Ricky's phones. We found them at the park in a trash bin."

Riley felt like she'd missed an entire inning of a game. "How are they communicating then?"

"Burner phones?" Rosita suggested. "This whole kidnapping thing feels sloppy, like a desperate grab, not planned out."

"I agree." Except for the AppleTag. That had been deliberate. Riley's phone dinged a text message. She saw that it was from Matthew and stepped away from the counter.

You back?

Riley tapped quickly. **Yes.**

The tourists in your office saw something that may or may not fit around the time Dante was taken from the park. Hunter and Mary Jo were on the search party but buying drugs and so didn't want to come forward. I told them we wouldn't press charges if they were honest.

That was par for the course—one hand washing the other. Riley hummed and typed, **Got it. What did they say?**

They saw a man leaving the park with a little boy on his hip. That's all. I'd hoped you might get more detail. I was making them nervous.

Thanks Matthew! And Dante?

I'm searching the pier by foot, but nothing so far. The cousins did not rent a boat from our marina, BTW.

Damn it. Riley entered her office where two barely-legal-drinking-age tourists dozed, as if they'd had a long night. She could relate. She cleared her throat, and they jumped alert.

The taller, thinner blond in his tie-dye shirt and denim cutoffs could have been Kurt Cobain on a bad day. His partner, shorter and not so emaciated, also a blonde, wiped her mouth with the back of her hand.

"Hey," Riley said, putting a softer tone into her voice. "Hunter and Mary Jo, right?" At their nod she continued playing nicely. "Officer Sniders said you guys were being cooperative and came down to talk with us about what you saw yesterday?"

"That redhead dude? He's too young to be a cop," the woman said. Her vocal cords had a scratchy note to them as if she smoked, a lot.

"You think? He has ten years' experience and is a decorated officer," Riley said, reminding herself to be patient. "He asked that I go lightly on you about the drug situation in the park. This is a zero-tolerance area, even for weed."

The young man's eyes lowered to the desk. There was nothing in her office worth stealing, and he was welcome to her stash of mints in the middle drawer. The desktop computer was outdated and old fashioned, though it served her purpose.

"He said we wouldn't get in trouble," Mary Jo countered, half-rising to leave.

Riley shook her head. "You must have got him on a good day. What is it you saw yesterday?"

"A boy who matches the description of the missing kid. His picture is all over the park. So yeah, I guess we saw Dante Catalina," Mary Jo said, wrinkling her nose.

"What time was this?" Riley took a seat opposite her desk, letting the two witnesses stay where they were.

Casual, relaxed, just shooting the breeze.

"We know it was one o'clock," Hunter said. "That was our appointment to meet with our friend."

Dealer. "Was Dante alone?" The last time Dante had been seen was around twelve thirty.

"No, he was being carried by a bigger guy. Maybe six feet, with light-brown hair," Mary Jo said. "Funny thing is he acted embarrassed by the kid throwing a temper tantrum. Oh, and the little boy was crying," she added. "But he was probably just being a brat for all we know."

Her boyfriend nodded.

"What did the man do?" Riley's skin was electric. Who the

hell was this guy? It didn't match the descriptions of the Russo and Esposito family. In pictures of Gino, it was obvious that he had dark hair.

"He told the kid that he was taking him for a ride on a boat and his mother would meet with them later." Mary Jo wiped the tip of her nose. Riley could guess her drug of choice. "It didn't look like he had much to say about it."

Forced by a stranger, he must have been terrified. Maybe too frightened to call for help. "Where was this in the park?"

"Oh, we weren't at the park. The marina."

Riley's stomach curdled. "What was Dante wearing, do you remember?"

Hunter squinted then said, "Nothing special. You know red, white, and blue tee, shorts, don't remember the color. When the boy started up a fuss, I remember the dude lost his grip but managed to grab the little boy's foot before he could get away. It made him angry. Told him to stop kicking. Yeah, that was strange for a dad to do, right?"

Both Hunter and Mary Jo were blondes. But they had no motive or love for children, that was obvious. For that matter Gino could have worn a wig.

"Did you kidnap Dante? Needing drug money by chance?"

"No!" Mary Jo said immediately.

"Hell no," Hunter seconded. "Where did you come up with that crazy idea?"

Riley couldn't tolerate another second with this druggy duo. "If you remember anything else—even if you don't think it's important, it might be, so give us a call. Cases are funny that way."

The pair looked at each other and then shook their heads.

"Hmm." Riley understood what Matthew meant...they weren't being entirely honest. She stood and channeled her inner warrior. "I've been interrogating folks for a great many years and sense that you're holding something back." She stared at them long enough to make them nervous. "Look, if you don't tell me everything, then I will toss you both in jail, and not honor my partner's deal, got it?"

Mary Jo turned as pale as snow. Her boyfriend squeezed her knee. Still, she yelped and said, "We have to help! That boy was sobbing for his mommy and tried to bite the bad man's hand. Earned a slap for it, but the kid just pounded his back and wouldn't stop. We left right after that."

CHAPTER FOURTEEN

Riley's stomach clenched and her pulse skyrocketed. The only excuse for these cold-blooded morons was that they were dropped on their heads as infants. She could barely look at them without revealing her disgust.

"You are here now and if you don't want to spend the night being drilled by the FBI and getting arrested for hindering an investigation then I suggest you start talking. Every word and action they made needs to come from your mouths." Riley forced a calm tone. "And don't lie. One special agent named Stephan is the size of a giant, and man-o-man does he have a mean temper."

As a mother and decent human, Riley wanted to rip their heads off. Reluctantly she had to remain professional and bite back the knowledge that if they'd lifted a finger or told someone right away, Dante would be home and the perpetrator in jail. Her fists curled and she did some yoga breaths to maintain control.

When they didn't immediately respond, she inhaled for the count of four and exhaled slowly. Her rage receded slightly.

"How could you look the other way?" Riley choked on her words.

"We didn't want to get involved, or miss our meeting," the scrawny blonde glanced at her boyfriend for confirmation.

"Right. We thought it was the dad at first; later we figured it was better to just look the other way." Hunter shrugged.

"Better for you, you mean!" Riley snapped. "Obviously you had a messed-up childhood, or you'd have done something to protect the boy." Disbelief pulsed through her veins. "I can't imagine anyone seeing a child mishandled and screaming for help without stepping in to protect the kid. Was your hook-up worth it?"

"You can't talk to us like this!" Hunter's face reddened. "We came down here to help, not get insulted. We don't like your attitude. Not one bit." He edged up closer to Riley and she hoped he'd do something stupid, not dangerous, but enough for her to bust him and lock them up in a small cell. Stephan could interrogate them all night long.

"I can and I will talk anyway I see fit. My name is Officer Riley Harper and this is my badge number." Riley pointed to her chest. "Want me to write it down?" She attempted to hold back her smirk. Wisely, the gangly young man stepped back, shooting a worried look at his love match.

"Yeah, okay. I get why you're mad," Hunter mumbled. "We didn't have nothin' to do with it though."

"Fine. This is your last chance." The nervous couple had dropped their eyes to stare at their shoes. Guilt and shame flashed over both faces. "Tell me what happened after the man slapped the boy and dragged him off as the boy fought for his life."

Tears filled Mary Jo's eyes and she swatted them away. Maybe the young girl had feelings after all and was acting tough to impress her boyfriend. Riley decided to drill her and leave Hunter alone. For now.

"Mary Jo, could you describe the assailant? Any unusual tats or something else that stood out?"

The young woman shook her head, gnawing on her bottom lip. Visibly shaking, Mary Jo rocked back and forth in her brown leather sandals and used her hand to wipe her nose.

Riley grabbed a few tissues from the desk and offered them to her. If this was her own daughter, she would want that person to show a little kindness.

Hunter put a hand on Mary Jo's back and answered the question. "Look, that scared the crap out of us, so we gathered our things and headed for the pier where we texted our source. That's it. We don't know anything after that."

Riley noticed how he avoided eye contact, and the tick in his jaw was a dead giveaway that he was lying.

"Mary Jo, do you have anything to add?"

"No. That's all we know, but if it helps, I couldn't sleep. I thought about that poor boy all through the night." Mary Jo waited with expectant eyes for Riley's approval, which wasn't coming.

As Riley was about to answer, C.C. walked in. Grateful to see him she blurted, "These two morons witnessed Dante being forcibly held and led away near the marina, not the park. Everything's recorded, don't worry." She waved her hand. "Sorry I can't be more help, but I need a break."

Not waiting for an answer, Riley stepped outside the front of the station and leaned against her SUV. She gulped fresh air. How to get the visions out of her head? If Dante didn't make it home, would that young couple ever forgive themselves? Depending on how high they got, they might not even care.

She called the house, needing to hear her daughter and her mom's upbeat voices to restore her faith in humanity. They were on Speaker, so she didn't have to relay this information twice.

"I will be home later tonight but until I am I want you both to be careful. Don't answer the door or pick up the phone unless you know it's me. I'm unnerved about you heading outdoors until we find Dante and the louse who took him."

"Mom, we're not going anywhere. I'm scared to death and can't stop worrying and crying over him. Nana too."

"I'm so sorry. Figured we'd have Dante home tonight, but it could take longer." Riley sighed deeply. "I'm more motivated than ever to get our boy back and put this monster in prison."

After their goodbyes, Riley re-entered the station and noticed that C.C. was still grilling Hunter and Mary Jo. He had a shorter temper than she did, so she left it to him and marched down the hall to the breakroom.

It wasn't long before C.C. joined her, having had the pair of stoners fingerprinted before leaving. "Did they have anything of importance to add?" she asked.

"Hell no—though they practically ran out of here. Hunter admitted to a prior drug bust that Mary Jo was unaware of and it didn't go over well. I told them that the interrogation was strictly confidential and not to do anything stupid like sell the story to the press. Unless they liked the idea of an all-expenses paid stay in the island jail."

Riley laughed when he told her this, and damn it felt good. "What should we tell Maria? She must be going crazy. Does she need to know about our visit to her cousins' hotel room?"

"Let's hold off," C.C. said. "Gather more information." He pulled out his tablet and read his notes. "Jessica saw Maria through the window and panicked. She couldn't face her and admit that she'd given Ricky and Marco the passcode. After the rejection from Coby, she'd intended to take the money which the cousins paid her and off she'd go, putting Sandpiper Bay in her rearview mirror. Or she could be a great actress and playing us both."

"You sound cynical," Riley said. "My gut says Jessica was approached by the cousins and fed a line about Maria having all this stolen money that belonged to them. Or the mafia, whatever. Anyway, they figured Maria had made a fool out of them. They were angry and wanted payback. An arrangement was made, and Jessica was caught in the crossfire."

"So, does she know Gino? If she doesn't then we need to find Ricky and Marco before they hightail it off island."

"Agreed. I'll contact Wyatt to post a guard at the ferry depot." Riley sipped from her now-cold coffee. "We have a footprint outside Maria's back door, and two from the break-in at Piazza Pizza. Hopefully one of those will be a match."

C.C. closed his tablet and stuck it back in his pocket. "What's the plan?"

"I thought that was my line," Riley teased. "Well, we should enter this new information on the board. Do we have anything else?"

"Not much." The agent scrubbed his chin. "Who do you think tossed Marco's room?"

"Gino," Riley said immediately. "He's around here somewhere and hasn't traveled by ferry. What if he's in disguise, and wearing a wig?" She turned toward C.C. "With all the big bucks he's making he can afford a luxury boat. So, where is he hiding it? And Dante?"

"Wish I had an answer. Hopefully Matthew will walk in with some good news." C.C. glanced at her. "Any decent cop knows the perpetrator always stays behind to admire his work. In this case he won't let Maria out of sight. His interest is the millions of mafia money that needs to be accounted for. I'm sure his neck is also on the line."

The enforcer being enforced? "That's it! We can lure Gino out of hiding. With Marie's help. I'm sure she'd want to be proactive in saving her beloved child, the light of her life."

"What are you thinking?" C.C. rubbed his hands together. "I'm chopping at the bit."

"Off the top of my head, this plan might bring Dante home

and keep the cousins away from Maria. Gino will get his take and the mafia their millions. Win, Win."

As Riley and C.C. brainstormed together, she knew this was a manageable strategy that could be arranged before nightfall. All they needed was for the key players to cooperate and everyone would smell like a rose.

C.C. left her to speak privately with Chief Barnes about this new idea and although there was no guarantee of success, it was worth a try. Dante needed them.

Riley was agitated and wanted to get the show on the road, yet everyone had to be on board. There could be no leaks, only complete silence until the deed was done. She kept glancing at her phone, counting the minutes since C.C. had left, practically wearing a hole in the cheap hallway carpet.

Suddenly the station was buzzing with activity. How could it be one already? The tantalizing scent of coffee and donuts, no not donuts, but sweet-smelling cinnamon rolls, added instant energy. Riley hurried toward the front desk. Rosita had an open cardboard box filled with treats that she'd placed on the counter.

"Hi." Rosita dropped her handbag on the counter next to the box. "Thought I'd stop for refreshments before coming in."

"Rosita! You're a gem. So nice of you to help out on a Sunday like this."

"I'm happy to assist in any way I can." Rosita hooked her thumb toward Barnes' office where C.C. and the chief were conversing. "Was there anything specific he needed me to do?"

"You'll have to ask Barnes...did you get the notes in the system from his interview with Jessica, or Mary Jo and Hunter?" Riley checked the time. Ten minutes after one. *Come on, C.C.!* "Feels like a fire has been lit under all of us today, wanting to bring Dante home. We know Gino Ferraro has him so it's just a matter of making a deal."

Rosita's expression grew hopeful. "Great news." Then in a

teasing voice she added a little salt to the wound. "I hear you had an exciting morning."

The embarrassing hotel room incident. Riley zipped her lips and waved C.C. forward as he left the chief's office. "It was interesting I've gotta say, but we don't have the cousins in custody yet. Right, Agent Craig?"

C.C. peered into the cardboard box of treats. "No, but we are making strides." He chose a small scone and took a large bite.

Matthew sauntered in and gave Rosita a smacking kiss on her cheek. "You're my new favorite person. Can I marry you?"

Rosita laughed and bumped his hip. "I'm waiting for you to grow up."

Matt laughed and gave her a side hug then offered his services. Rosita nodded and handed him the box of cinnamon rolls. Riley held the large bowl of cut fruit, and C.C. grabbed the assorted goodies as they all paraded down to the breakroom.

Barnes had come out of his office after smelling the food, seemingly in a jovial mood. Riley ached to talk to him. Would he approve the idea or shut it down? She knew she'd have to wait until after lunch to question him.

Rosita and Matthew laid out the plates and assembled the tray of fresh pastries, blueberry muffins, croissants, plus the cinnamon rolls, in the center of the long wooden table.

Stephan burst into the back room in time for the impromptu lunch. Elizabeth and Jeff had returned in the helo as well. C.C. stood next to her, and Matthew flanked her other side.

"A feast!" Stephan declared.

Riley smiled at Rosita and pointed in her direction. "Our kind and thoughtful Rosita did all this, so let's give her a moment's appreciation before we start digging in like the wolves we are."

A quick round of applause got things rolling as the officer's dove in. Riley watched her phone for any notifications from Kyra or Maria.

After her cinnamon roll and fruit, body fueled, Riley stood and made eye contact with those still eating and chatting. Where there had been expressions of dissatisfaction prior to the break, the team was now alert and ready for action. "Thirty minutes is up. How about we finish what's on our plates and get back to the search? Dante must be scared to death." His fear galvanized her into motion.

Elizabeth dropped a napkin over her plate. "I'll go to the Drunken Pelican. I called but the front desk person said nobody by the cousin's names was registered."

Stephan stood with reluctance. "I'm on my way to Maria's, but dang, these are good."

Riley grabbed a roll from the basket and handed it to him. "There. Now go in peace."

He grinned and winked. "You're a softy at heart, but I'll keep the secret."

"Take that back," she snarled.

"I'll carry it to my grave." Stephan raised the fresh bread. "Good luck everyone."

Riley turned toward Barnes wondering what it would take to get his agreement. "Chief!" She gave him one of the remaining warm rolls. "Can we talk?"

∼

RILEY SAT IN BARNES' OFFICE AS HE GATHERED THE INFORMATION on the two tourists for Rosita to enter in the database. Not much there. Small stuff like selling weed. Hunter had been in a bar fight. Mary Jo worked in a strip joint.

Nothing suspicious or connected in any way to the cousins or Gino Ferraro.

Riley drummed her fingers on the office chair. "Where the hell has Gino gone? Where are the cousins? They can't leave without the money, or they'll be marked men. Please tell me you're on board with this quickly put-together plan?"

"Riley, I agree that you and C.C. devised a brilliant plan, but we need confirmation that Gino has Dante, alive, before I'll give my approval. We're not putting Maria in danger from a man who wants her dead without proof of Dante's life. No Dante, no millions. Right? Agent Craig agrees."

"This is so frustrating." Riley made two fists. "Chief, it's the most logical conclusion. The cousins said that Gino has Dante."

"The cousins are not reliable witnesses," Barnes said. "What else do we have?"

"I can try to track down the asshole who ran his fancy boat into the teens' dingy the night of July Fourth. He was probably just drunk, but he was fighting with a woman we assume is his wife, and who knows why he'd run off with a kid? Maybe he's a perp and wifey is not happy."

"Please, don't even go there." Barnes grabbed a tissue from a box by his computer and dotted the perspiration on his brow. "A man with an appetite for children would likely be on the FBI radar. C.C. seems convinced this is a 'normal,'" he used his fingers for emphasis, "abduction—probably for ransom, given the mob connection."

Riley sat back in the office chair, not willing to give up. "Look, we know the cousins came for the money. They didn't believe Maria when she told them she didn't have it, didn't want it, and only craved peace for herself and her son. They thought she'd hidden it somewhere on her property and they'd come to collect. After Dante went missing, she called and called, and they didn't pick up. Ricky and Marco assumed Gino had nabbed Dante and that they'd be cut out of the deal unless they reached the treasure first. Plot thickens, doesn't it?"

"Jessica said they wanted revenge against Maria for what they viewed as stolen money and combined with Coby's rejection; she made the bad decision to go along with it." Barnes rolled the tissue to a ball and tossed it in the trash. "Must've been a big disappointment when there was only a few thousand not the millions that they believed Maria inherited from her dad. So, they trashed her place."

Riley nodded. "I don't feel bad for Jessica; she should have known better. Getting involved with the likes of them. Because he chose Maria over her. I mean, really?"

Barnes sat back in his chair. "If one of my girls did that...but of course they wouldn't. They have better sense. Anyway, I too believe that Gino has Dante but hasn't contacted Maria because the FBI will nab him in an instant. Like one of those Mexican stand-offs. My suggestion to C.C. was that the FBI should back off a little, fade out of the picture so they would feel safe. Once we know for sure where Gino has Dante."

Riley propped her elbows on the armrests of the chair. "I wonder if the cousins are laying low, waiting for Gino to contact them. Can't we use them too? Sweeten the pot with some cash, or a deal? I'm sure dum and dummer would be agreeable."

Barnes exhaled loudly. "Fine. Go talk to Maria and have her suggest to Gino they should meet—someplace where they'd both be comfortable. Perhaps the lawyer's office in Brooklyn for their interaction. The FBI, all of us, will be there to greet him but completely hidden."

"Stephan is at Maria's right now." Riley was stoked that they were one step closer. After a pause she asked, "Chief? How long have you known Coby? Where did he come from? What's he doing on this isolated island...a young viral man with no other aspirations than owning a bar? I mean, did he give Jessica some kind of signal to let her think he was attracted and open?"

"I think Jessica is a troubled young woman." Barnes swung his chair around. "I know we're frustrated and scratching deep to uncover a clue to help us find Dante. Coby is solid and has integrity in every dealing I've had with him. I'd trust him with my life. However, I'm worried sick over that little boy. What if Gino decides he has no use for Dante? What's his next move?"

Riley closed her eyes and rubbed her arms, chilled to the core. It was two p.m. and over twenty-four hours had passed since the kidnapping. "What if we're too late?"

Chief Barnes tapped the desk to get her attention. "Riley. This is no time to fall apart. You're stronger than that and I put my faith in you. Between all the experience that we bring to the table, coupled with our FBI agents and the tools at their disposal, we will crack this case. Sooner than later. Agreed?"

"Agreed. I'm sorry. It's very personal because I keep hearing Kyra's guilt over losing track of Dante." How could they force Gino to take action? "All right. I'll go talk with Maria about working with her cousins, but if she agrees, can we set the plan in motion? I mean, it won't take much. Maria can make it publicly known that she's making a short trip to Brooklyn this evening and will return in the morning." Flights to Brooklyn from the island were less than two hours.

She had Barnes' attention. "Today? That's really fast. I don't want her in danger."

"She'd be accompanied by one or two undercover agents," Riley said, sticking to the plan she and C.C. had devised.

Barnes templed his fingers and leaned forward. "With another agent waiting at the other side. In fact, let's skip the lawyer and have her go straight to the bank."

"On a Sunday?"

"The FBI have connections beyond ours," the chief said.

Riley could see it playing out in her head and went along with the revision. "Yes! Maria should act like she's unaware of anything but getting to the bank for the money in the safe deposit box. Gino will fall into the trap."

"Where is Agent Craig?"

Riley hit the intercom, rarely used, since they usually raised their voices. "Agent Craig? You are summoned to Chief Barnes office," she said with a smile at Barnes.

Without knocking, C.C. stepped inside and listened carefully to the polished plan, then nodded his satisfaction. "I feel this might work. As long as Maria goes along with it, we'll make it happen." His phone rang. "It's Elizabeth—she went to check out the motel to find the cousins once she got back with Jeff. Jeff's refueling." He put the phone to his ear, listened, then placed the call on Speaker. "Say that again?"

"Ricky and Marco are staying at the Drunken Pelican like Jessica thought but under assumed names—Joe and Bobby Marino," Elizabeth said. "Shall I proceed?"

"Wait!" Riley said. She looked at C.C. Yes, she was a team player, but this was her island now and she and Matt deserved to be in the game when it came to catching the cousins and Dante.

C.C. gave her a nod. "Riley and I are on our way."

They smacked palms. "Payback for Ricky," Riley said. "He won't know what hit him." And they certainly owed the Russo cousin for his escape. They could charge him with shooting an officer and a federal agent.

"I'll talk with Maria," Barnes said.

CHAPTER FIFTEEN

Riley drove to the Drunken Pelican on the far side of the island in a little cove behind a hill. The view of rocks and scrub brush was awful. It was no wonder the dive didn't query the guests too hard about ID.

She texted Matthew a quick update then parked next to Elizabeth who'd borrowed the chief's SUV. "This was probably an old pirate hang out," Riley said.

"I can see it," C.C. agreed from the passenger seat.

They exited the vehicle at the same time as Elizabeth slipped out of hers. The agent wore leather boots, jeans, and a lightweight jacket over the holster visible at her side. She handed Riley a pair of binoculars. "They just left their room and headed toward the beach, hotel towels over their shoulders. Not much to look at," she smirked.

Riley looked across the road and could see two dark-haired men on the sand below. Ricky, the pudgy one, and Marco, the more fit of the pair. "I say we tackle them and bring them to their room for interrogation."

Elizabeth's brow winged upward. "Seriously?" She peered around Riley to C.C. "I like this chick."

"She's cool," C.C. agreed. "So, are we good with that plan?"

"Our goal is to get answers from them. Where is Gino, does he have Dante? That kind of thing." Riley gave an evil grin. "A little waterboarding if necessary."

"We'll ignore that last part," Elizabeth said. "I'll pull the SUV up to block the view of the beach to keep us from any gawkers. Just in case."

Riley grinned at Elizabeth. "Perfect. C.C.?" She nodded toward the hotel where she imagined questioning the cousins until they had the answers needed. The plus? It was so out of the way they hadn't hit any traffic on the road.

"Let's do it." C.C. lowered his shades from the top of his head to cover his eyes. "I call dibs on Ricky."

Riley moved as stealthy as a shadow until she was on the side of the street closest to the beach. C.C. stuck like a burr to her side. "Fine by me."

Scrub brush was the only plant that had thrived on this part of the coast. The Drunken Pelican was a faded cement block single-story structure with a wooden pelican listing to the side. By design or age, it was hard to tell. No cars at the hotel, just two rented bikes locked to the outdoor ice machine.

There was no hint of Dante. No sign of anyone but the dopey cousins. Knowing that the boy's fate was in Gino's hands did not sit well with her.

C.C. had his hand at his hip, just as Riley did, and they maneuvered down the rocky path. Behind them, Elizabeth parked the chief's SUV on the road. Part of the trail was blocked by rocks or bushes as it wound its way down the steep hill to the beach. Pebbles the size of her fist made it difficult to walk. Certainly not the French Riviera, but a fraction of the cost, she chuckled to herself.

Elizabeth moved silently behind them.

The cousins tossed a football back and forth on the rocky

beach. Riley stopped and put her hand to her lips in a signal to wait and listen.

Ricky was a chatterbox and talked about everything from missing his girlfriend to the shitty motel, and how Gino was going to pay.

Riley raised a brow at that. She didn't see how these two buffoons would make Gino Ferraro do anything. As an enforcer for the mob, Gino was much higher up in rank. As they threw the ball back and forth, Riley grew impatient.

"Shall we?" she whispered. "I'll take Marco, C.C. has Ricky."

Elizabeth grinned and pulled a round object from her jacket pocket. "I've got the duct tape."

"On the count of three," C.C. murmured.

The actual tackling of Marco Esposito was a let-down after the adrenaline high Riley had been on. He didn't give her any problems once she'd had him flipped onto his stomach in the sand, digging her knee in his back so that he didn't squirm.

Elizabeth was a whiz with heavy-duty silver tape; within minutes they had the guys up against the dirt hill. The deserted cove was a more obscure place to question them.

Ricky and C.C. each had a bloody lip from the scuffle as Ricky had fought hard not to be restrained. It was prison for him.

Elizabeth stepped back to stand guard so that the interview wasn't interrupted. She slapped a sharp knife against her palm. "There's more duct tape if you need it. Between that and rope, I don't know why anybody would ever use other tools."

The cousins cringed.

"Where is Dante?" Riley asked. She searched their faces for any sign of dishonesty.

"Gino has him," Ricky said. "And this is police brutality." He licked the small drop of blood from his lip.

"It would never stand up in court," Riley assured him. "You shot at us earlier today at the Sandpiper Bay Hotel. You're going to jail." She hovered her hand over the gun in her holster. "Why are you at this cheap dive?"

Marco grinned, his teeth yellow from smoking his cigars. "They don't ask no questions."

C.C. inched closer, a hint of five o'clock shadow on his chiseled jaw at two p.m. "Gino rifled your guys' hotel room at the hotel. We know you have a long history together. Where is Gino? Which one of you took Dante?"

"Why should we answer you?" Marco asked defiantly.

"Jail for you too, Marco, if you don't." Riley wasn't playing around.

"You are both two times in the system," Elizabeth added to the conversation. "Third time is the charm for Ricky already."

"How do we reach Gino?" C.C. asked. "Can you guys call him? Oh no, that's right. You busted your phones and we found them in the park." He shook his head.

"We got more," Marco said. "Don't matter. Just wait until we get home and Uncle Alphonso finds out about Maria. If Gino don't kill her, I bet he'll send a hit."

Ricky groaned. "Stupid idiot."

Riley would be amused at their bravado if only she knew where Dante was. She needed these goons to find him. "Why would Gino want to kill Maria?"

"Her dad stole from us. Gino's the enforcer. It's his job. Ain't personal." Marco struggled against the tape around his wrists and his ankles. "This is too tight."

"Stop moving," Elizabeth suggested.

"Good advice," C.C. said. He had his arms crossed, his weapon in the holster at his hip. He'd fought with Ricky, but it had been a fair fight. No shot in the back like her ex-partner.

Riley paced back and forth. "So. You guys have burner phones. Do you know Gino's number?"

"Nope," Ricky said, cutting off Marco. "He calls us—that's how it works."

"What about Maria? You thought she had the money, so why the sudden silence?" Riley really couldn't comprehend their unwillingness to get this over with.

"We watched Maria all of Friday," Marco said. "We had no clue she had a kid. So, after a few beers we figured we should call my uncle and tell him about it. He told us to sit tight. I think he was letting Gino know."

"Did you put the AppleTag in Maria's purse at the funeral?" Riley asked. Maria had been so clever, but she'd been busted by technology.

"Our grandmother Russo." The cousins smiled at one another.

And her family. Maria had been taken down by family ties.

In order to catch a rat, sometimes you needed cheese. In this instance, Maria could be considered high-end Brie.

"We'd like to make a deal," Riley said sharply. "Not that you deserve it…either of you."

She glanced at C.C. who added, "It's a onetime only get-out-of-jail free card."

"Huh? You're kidding aren't cha?" Marco shook his head. "Wish we could accept the offer, but our family don't do deals. Cops can't be trusted."

C.C. moved next to Riley and faced the cousins. "I think they might approve of this one. How would you like that money Maria's dad stole?"

The cousins exchanged looks. "What do you mean?" Ricky asked with a wary tone.

"*Only* if you agree. And if Maria will go along with it. But she'd do anything to get her son back," Riley spoke in a cool voice, hating that these two might end up free. If Dante had been harmed at all, she'd want payback. "Oh, never mind."

Riley turned her back to the cousins still tied with tape. Elizabeth was a genius. The stuff was easy to pack and the more they struggled the tighter the bond. "Can we use your chopper to fly to Brooklyn?" she asked Elizabeth, realizing she hadn't been brought up to speed with that part of the plan. "It would be the fastest way to get all three of them there."

Elizabeth looked doubtful. "The helo isn't a taxi service."

C.C. nudged her arm. "It's not orthodox but it is the most direct route to Dante."

At that, Elizabeth relented. "I'll talk to Jeff."

Riley nodded. "Thanks. I'm very curious as to how the conversation went with Barnes and Maria."

C.C. wiped his puffy lip. "I feel like we've moved a giant step closer to finding Dante but yet he's still out of reach."

Letting the cousins steam, the agents admired the beautiful day and all the boats on the water for a good ten minutes.

"We want to talk," Marco said at last.

Riley exhaled with relief and the three officers turned around again. "You can get up now," C.C drawled.

Ricky and Marco stumbled to their feet.

"If you jokers mess up, it will be doomsday." Riley patted her holster, not releasing Marco from her gaze until he nodded.

Elizabeth went up the steep trail first, sheathing her knife. Still no traffic on this deserted cove.

Riley settled Marco in the back with C.C. riding shotgun next to her. Ricky was in the chief's SUV. Elizabeth had sliced through the tape at Ricky's wrists and exchanged it for handcuffs after cuffing Marco. "See you there," Elizabeth said.

With the radio blaring, Riley and C.C. discussed the plans in quiet voices so Marco couldn't hear. Fifteen minutes later, they arrived at the station.

C.C. and Marco went inside, Marco's hands behind his back. Elizabeth gently pushed Ricky toward the door. For some reason Ricky didn't seem too eager to enter the Sandpiper Bay police station. Riley couldn't blame him for being cautious. There were consequences for breaking the law and shooting at officers. The cousins were stashed in Riley's office—which used to be a storage area before her arrival.

"Hey." Barnes met them at the reception counter. "I didn't leave yet. There's some pushback from the higher-ups about Maria being used as a target."

"Okay." Riley was disappointed at the slow pace of justice. For every step forward there were several more backward. "I'll talk to her...I still think it's the best way and the cousins might be swayed for a deal to keep Ricky from jail."

"We'll finetune the plan with Barnes and see about getting past that resistance," C.C. said fervently.

Time was ticking. Riley couldn't stop tapping the leather wheel during the short drive to Maria's house. Stressed, she needed movement. Dante had to come home.

Riley parked on the sidewalk and the door swung open. Stephan waved at her, looking relieved by her arrival. His shirt was wet. He'd been expecting her as Elizabeth had made contact and gotten him up to date.

"Maria's been sleeping this whole time," Stephan said. "I'd like to run back to the station and change—had an accident with the kitchen faucet. Thought I'd fix a drip and instead remembered that I'm not a plumber."

"Here." Riley handed him the key to her car. "No problem." He was a good guy, despite his temper.

"Thanks. I'll be back in a flash. Coby's got the pipe situation handled."

"All right." Riley walked in and announced herself. "Hey!"

Coby came to greet her, wiping his hands on a dish towel. "Riley—any news of Dante?"

"Not yet, but we have an idea that is going to take some finessing." Riley noticed his mouth was puffy, like C.C.'s lip. "What happened?"

"Maria totally lost it and attacked me while I was taking a nap on the couch." Coby touched his swollen lip.

"What?"

"I know she's going through hell, but she's convinced I'm having an affair with Jessica and was involved in Dante's abduction." Eyes wild with fear, Coby started to pace the hallway. "You know I'm not, right? I love Maria very much, and Dante. I want us to be a family, but she always turns me down. Yet I'm still here, because she's the best person I've ever known, and I won't let her push me away."

"You're a good man, Coby. Deep down Maria knows it." Riley scanned the kitchen, then the living room for Maria but didn't see her exhausted friend. "Is she still sleeping? I wanted to tell her that Jessica was the one who gave the cousins the passcode."

"What did you just say?" Maria staggered in from the bedroom wearing a long-sleeved T-shirt down to her knees. Her hair was knotted and needed a good wash. Her eyes were swollen into dark holes. Coby rushed to her side, holding her against him to keep her upright.

"I'm so sorry. Jessica gave Marco and Ricky the passcode to the restaurant and told them to look under your keyboard for the code to the safe. Barnes interviewed her then released her, but she remains a person of interest and was told not to leave the island. She feels terrible about it, Maria. I believe she's sincere."

Maria staggered backward. "Why would she do this to me?"

"Jessica was jealous of the love Coby has for you and wanted to hurt you. As for your cousins, they are in custody at the station right now. They want the money your dad stole. Also, Gino wants that too." Riley said softly, "He has Dante."

Maria's knees buckled. "No. No! Why?"

"Gino doesn't want Dante and I'm pretty damn sure that he's in no physical danger. Since he's the enforcer for the mob if he doesn't get that money, he'll be the one dead. It's you he wants, but with the FBI here he can't make his move."

"So, take me to Gino!" Maria fell to her knees. "Take me. Give me Dante."

"I have a plan," Riley said. "You aren't going to like it."

Coby helped Maria to her feet. She eyed Riley with suspicion. How to get her to agree? It was easy to get the cousins on board, as Riley and C.C. had threatened jail and offered access to Maria's inheritance.

Maria pushed away from Coby, heading for the couch. "I have no more to say to you Riley Harper, until you bring Dante back to me." She slumped onto the sofa and Coby sat next to her, holding her hand.

"I have something to ask you and I'm glad Coby is here. We have an idea how to bring Gino out in the open and believe this will work."

"What?"

"You have to go to Brooklyn with your cousins."

"Absolutely not." Maria looked at Riley as if she'd lost her mind.

In as few words as possible she told them what the FBI agents, Chief Barnes, and Riley had discussed. Riley also mentioned that Matthew was in deep with another lead, and they hadn't had a chance to catch up yet.

"We all believe we can get your son back *if* you cooperate." Riley watched Maria go through every scenario she could imagine. Fear never once left her face. "And you will always be guarded by an undercover agent."

For the next thirty minutes, Maria and Coby asked the questions and Riley filled in the details.

The couple locked hands and Maria smiled for the first time since the abduction. "Okay."

Riley smiled too. "They want to do this ASAP. First, we need to get the word out there that you're going to Brooklyn later today. The news will spread fast, especially with a little help from our friends."

"Today? It's half over?" Maria asked. She brought her hand to her tangled hair.

"Agent Craig will be calling soon and when you give your permission he'll come over and run you right through it."

Coby and Maria stood up and thanked her. Maria patted her head. "I need to shower! You answer the phone if it rings, Coby. Tell them I'm getting ready for my trip."

Riley sagged with relief. She looked at Coby, who was very worried. "It will be okay." Sure, there was a ton that could go wrong. When compared to Dante's life, this was worth the risk of taking on the mob.

∼

WHEN BOARDED ON THE FBI CHOPPER, THE CHAIN OF COMMAND differed. Jeff and Elizabeth were in charge of the actual flight, and C.C., Matthew, and Riley guarded Maria and kept the cousins under control. Stephan and the chief were homebase. As they lifted in the air, Riley let out a breath. It was five o'clock on a Sunday and she hadn't seen her daughter and mom for more than a few hours in days. She wanted this over.

Matthew had understood why he hadn't been in the loop and explained that he'd been trying to find Hunter and Mary Jo's dealer to see if he might have noticed anything to point them in the right direction. He'd asked the Tylers if they might hypnotize Shane to see if he could remember the name of the boat. He was thrilled to join the team to bring Dante home.

Ricky and Marco sat next to each other; all pepped up as they took selfies inside the helo with their burner phones. When C.C. yelled at them to settle down and shut up, he also reminded them why they were here and the calls they had yet to make. Still in high spirits they pointed at each other with silly grins on their faces.

Riley sat two seats behind, with Maria across from her, and

noticed that the cousins were not dumb enough to ignore C.C.'s command.

Marco's job was to call Alphonso and smooth his uncle's feathers. He gave him an update and reassured him that they had everything under control. Ricky tried Gino's number but got no response. He had it on speed dial.

Maria didn't need a warning. She nodded to Riley and dialed the bank manager, Harvey Smith, the man C.C. had suggested that Riley contact, and reminded him of the meeting for seven thirty that night. "We're on schedule."

Riley had stressed the need for privacy as well as her position, and the FBI's backing. She'd paid a bonus for Mr. Smith to come in on a Sunday night.

Ricky kept Riley in the loop, letting her know that Gino was ignoring their calls. She could see that they were both worried that Gino would not show up with Dante—and blow the deal they'd made with the FBI to keep Ricky out of jail for shooting at a federal agent. The main lure was the money that Maria had inherited.

During the two-hour flight Riley noticed Maria's agitation. If this exchange didn't go through Maria would fall to pieces. Maria unbuckled her seatbelt and Riley hoped the woman had to use the restroom. But no.

Maria, looking like a supermodel with her black suit and heels, glorious hair down around her waist, stopped before Marco and Ricky, crossing her arms, chin jutted. Her confident appearance was blown by her shaking knees.

"What?" Ricky said with a smirk.

"If anything goes wrong, you will regret coming to my island. Right now, I'd give almost anything to open the window and throw both of you out like trash. You have no reason to be on this earth… and I will never forgive you for letting Gino know where I lived."

Marco rumbled a curse. C.C., Riley, and Matthew all perked up to hear the conversation.

"We didn't know Gino would take the kid," Ricky said. "He was supposed to find out where you had hidden the money. That's all."

"You better pray that Gino hasn't harmed my son because if he has you will never see the light of day. Gangbangers will have a field day with you." Maria's voice was chilling. "I told you that I didn't know about my dad skimming money. And I sure don't want it. You all can have it and burn in hell as far as I'm concerned."

"If you'd told us this at the funeral this never would have happened," Marco said. "It's your fault your son was taken!"

Maria gasped and swayed in her high-heeled shoes. Then she began punching both of them who cowered in their seats, hands covering their heads. C.C. hauled the irate mother off her cousins.

"Enough! This will all be over soon, so let's just settle down." C.C. walked back to his seat.

Maria hissed to her cousins, "After the funeral I went to the lawyer's, and I knew you were there. I smelled Marco's stinky cigar. So, I left quickly."

"Big mistake," Ricky drawled from the corner of his mouth.

"You both disgust me with your greed and lack of humanity. But why am I surprised?" Maria panted with rage.

"Chill out," Marco answered. "Once we get the money and hand it over to Gino, we'll be square."

Maria whispered, "I would give everything up to have Dante in my arms right now. When this is over, I never want to see your ugly faces or hear from you again."

Ricky bowed his head. "You will get your wish, and to clear the air we didn't know what Gino had planned."

"I'm tired of this bullshit. You know Gino, and what kind of man he is," Maria shouted. "He's capable of anything, even murder, if it saved his hide."

"I'm sure he just wanted to get you riled up enough to do whatever he asked. You know him and his big ego," Marco said. "The Enforcer. The money man."

"Gino is pure evil. Jeez, my dad's been gone not even a month." Maria's voice cracked. "I'm sure he's churning in his grave."

"His dying had nothing to do with us," Ricky said. "We might have pressured him a little, but he had no use for the money, and we needed it to keep the mob from ripping us in half."

"What I'll never understand is why you were on the island and never made contact with me? It makes no sense. I know you were here a full day before my Dante was taken," she hissed. "If one hair on my baby's head is even ruffled, you all better run for the hills." Maria threw them a long last glance that could have frozen a lion's heart.

Riley, within hearing distance, wanted to cheer.

"Uncle Alphonso told us not to answer you," Marco said.

In tears, Maria returned to her original seat and stared out the window. Riley decided to let her be. She'd needed to confront them and unleash her anger. Only when she had Dante again would she begin to heal.

When they arrived in Brooklyn, they grabbed two taxis to take them to the large gray financial structure that towered over the smaller buildings and shops. C.C. and Elizabeth rode with Maria; the agents wore casual clothes and caps, blending into the background. Their weapons were well concealed.

Riley was wearing a dress and sandals, her gun safely hidden under the pashmina tossed over her shoulders. She was the handler for Ricky and Marco, who were on their best behavior.

The meeting with Harvey Smith went smoothly. Maria was escorted to the vault where she emptied out the belongings, barely glancing at the stocks, bonds, and investments that her father had collected over the years. He had turned the first million dollars of his dirty money into legit finance which the mob couldn't touch, leaving other millions to be fought over.

Gold and silver in dark red velvet pouches had belonged to her mother, as well as the ring Maria held up to admire.

"It's beautiful," Riley said.

"My mom's."

The banker coughed and turned his back, allowing them privacy. Maria slipped the jewelry into her small handbag, restored the remaining items to the vault before nodding at Riley. "This is all I want. I'm ready."

They stepped into the elevator Mr. Smith held open. In less than a minute they were in the lobby on the first floor.

"Now, next door at the restaurant," Riley said. "You're doing great, Maria."

"I just want Dante." Maria's face was pale.

"I know." Riley opened the restaurant door and followed a hostess to a private room where the Russo and Esposito families waited. They wore their Sunday best as this was a high-end eatery Alphonso had reserved.

Riley wondered if they were on the take or knew the dinner would be expensed by the FBI.

This was to be the meeting place for Gino to make the exchange—Dante for the key to the vault which she'd just authorized.

Gino wasn't there. Alphonso made frantic calls which were ignored. The families ordered a couple of bottles of their best champagne, escargot for everyone as well as a platter of calamari. Dinner was to be delayed until Gino arrived, and Dante returned.

An hour passed, and the meal was at last served. Riley and Maria sat at a private table where Maria did more drinking than eating. "He's torturing me," Maria whispered.

The first course was devoured by Ricky, Marco, and their

family while C.C. and Elizabeth picked at their food, keeping their eyes sharp and conversation low. Matthew and Jeff surveyed the entrance, out of sight.

C.C. texted Riley to alert her that he'd called the local FBI and police, ordering them to arrest Gino Ferraro and contact them immediately. Maria shoved aside her untouched lasagna. Riley forced herself to eat a bite or two, to maintain the façade.

The sound of laughter and celebration going on behind them made Riley sick to her stomach. She wanted to have them thrown out and might have if Gino didn't slide in from the direction of the kitchen unnoticed by the agents in the front. She was not overly surprised that they had chosen a hangout for the mob. Still, it made her skin crawl.

The family members greeted Gino, clapping his shoulders, and giving him hugs.

Maria broke down in sobs. Dante wasn't with her tormentor. She started to rise.

"Wait!" Riley texted C.C. and the others that Gino had slipped into the private room via the kitchen. She stood in front of her friend. Gino was slick, his eyes bright with malice as he reached for Maria and yanked her hair.

Riley chopped her palm to his wrist, and he let go, spinning his evil gaze toward her. Maria whimpered from behind. It was no wonder she'd been afraid for her life.

C.C. and Elizabeth raced inside, and C.C. had Gino handcuffed as Elizabeth read Gino his rights.

Gino didn't flinch, knowing they couldn't pin anything on him. "Maria!" He smiled like a serpent.

C.C. had the butt of a gun pressed hard against his back, making Gino's knees buckle.

"Where's the boy," C.C. growled.

"Don't know," Gino grimaced.

Maria wiped away her tears and stood, her chin trembling. Riley patted her arm as a reminder that she was not alone.

"You piece of shit! Where is Dante?" Maria flew at him, her nails scratching his face. He spat at her. And Riley slid out her gun. Oh, how she wanted to use it.

Maria wiped the spit off with a cloth from the table and whipped around with a bottle in one hand, staring him down. "I've got the key and the money which you will never see if you don't tell us right now where Dante is."

"Can't tell you what I don't know."

Maria smashed the bottle, threatening him with it. "If you want to play this game, I'm sure the FBI will enjoy the moment too."

C.C. gritted his teeth and bent Gino in half.

"You want to play?" C.C. wrenched his arms and increased the pressure. "Cause I'm in the mood. You better start talking and stop stalling."

Gino stumbled as C.C. dropped his hands. "You guys taping this? Police brutality. I won't start talking until you remove the cuffs. I'm an innocent man."

C.C. glanced at Elizabeth and nodded. Elizabeth removed the cuffs and stood back. Gino wasn't going anywhere, except maybe to prison. Riley noticed Jeff blocking the entrance to the kitchen while Matt guarded the other doorway.

"I don't have your son. Never did. The money is the only thing that I came for, and now I mean to collect."

"He's telling the truth," Maria said in an empty voice. "God help me."

Gino brushed past C.C., taunting him as he sneered at Maria.

Elizabeth put her leg out, effectively stopping him from taking another step.

"What do you want to do with him?" Elizabeth asked her fellow agent.

"We'll turn him over to the local police until we have Dante back alive," C.C. said. "Then we'll let the judges decide what to do with this habitual criminal. A long stint in a federal prison might be the ticket."

With that, C.C. and Elizabeth took sides and shuffled Gino out the door as Matthew stepped aside.

The silence in the private room was deafening until the family erupted with questions and accusations. Riley assisted Maria out through the lobby to the sidewalk.

"This sucks," Matt said.

"Yeah." Riley put her arm around Maria.

Dante was not coming home tonight.

CHAPTER SIXTEEN

Head down and angrier than hell, Riley and her fellow officers boarded the helo which was light two passengers but heavy in heart.

Riley called Barnes to give him the crippling news. "Gino Ferraro doesn't have Dante Catalina. We're on our way back to the station."

"Damn it." Barnes hung up.

Curses abounded and fists were raised. Riley felt their collective angst as the conclusion they'd hoped for fell apart. Dante wouldn't be returned to his mother, and the FBI agents couldn't move on to their next case. Maria and Coby would not have Dante and until they did their life was shattered.

Riley held Maria's hand on the flight back as the woman sobbed quietly, facing away from her. She had added her mother's ring to her many bands and used her finger to slide it back and forth, back and forth, swaying as she did so. She seemed in a trance, a mindless place where there was no pain, no missing child, just a deep ache in her heart. She mumbled a little, placing her head on the side of the helo with no window. Blessedly she fell into a deep slumber, a healing place where she could rest.

Riley slipped away as a new thought ran through her head. "Matthew, you were right to concentrate on the marina! The druggies said that they'd seen the light-haired man with a boy at the marina near one. That means the abductor had time from the bubble machine to go to the Catalina home. The Tyler family also saw a light-haired man."

Elizabeth was up stretching her legs and heard the excitement in Riley's words. She stopped and looked back at Maria who was stirring. She put a finger to her mouth to let the others know to keep this quiet for now.

Until they knew anything further Maria was better sleeping.

And yet Maria surprised them. Standing up she scrubbed her cheeks and walked toward the cockpit, weaving just a little. "A light-haired man? The only one I know is Coby. Coby wouldn't hurt Dante."

"Of course, he wouldn't. He loves you both so much." Riley put a hand on her friend's back. "We have to search for a light-haired man who did, by taking Dante."

Silence fell over the group. Who would hurt a child? Nobody Riley knew on the island.

Maria paled. "The man I had a brief affair with seven years ago had sandy-brown hair. Light but not blond, like Coby. It couldn't be him because we haven't been in contact since I called his number and his wife answered." She sniffed and put her hand in her pocket to retrieve a tissue. "He was such a nice person and offered to pay me support. I refused, but how many married men would do that?" In a weak voice, she added, "He was only at my home a couple of times, and I doubt that he'd remember the house number. Besides, he has no idea if I'm still here or carried his child to term."

"When he had visited you, did he take the ferry?" Riley asked.

"No. No! He had his own boat." Maria's chin trembled.

"Did his boat have a name?"

"I have no idea," Maria said with exasperation.

Sandy-haired man who owned a boat. Riley dialed Barnes. "Hey, Chief. How about calling the Tyler family to see if they remember anything else about the boat that destroyed their dingy? Matthew and I feel that the two incidences might be related." She gave her partner a thumbs-up.

"Yeah, sure."

"Also, how did the Nathan White lead turn out?"

"No information, yet. It's possible that the name he gave wasn't real—if a man is a cheater, he's not likely to be honest. Now, tell me exactly what happened with Gino?"

"He showed up at the restaurant alone. No Dante. Said he didn't take him and doesn't know where the kid is. The worst thing is that I believe him—so did Maria. Meanwhile, Ricky and Marco walk free."

Barnes sighed deeply. "Crap. Back to square one, is that what you're telling me?"

"Not exactly. We have the boat angle, the Nathan White thread, and the sandy-haired man," Riley said.

"Let me talk to Special Agent Craig."

Riley handed C.C. the phone and took a seat behind Maria, worried about her but needing alone time to go through everything they knew and what they had missed. The agent returned it moments later.

On her phone app, Riley reread her files and notes. If the obvious criminals had not taken Dante, then who had? A charming youthful man who'd be friendly and persuasive. Someone who could fly under the radar. Not a local but an outsider who'd been lurking around at the scene of the crime, an opportunist who knew how to lure a child away with promises and deceit. The worst type of individual without a conscience or remorse.

She'd cracked many a case similar to this in her hey-day in Phoenix when she'd been at the top of her game. She closed her eyes for a moment, remembering how far she had fallen, the apology letter, the offer to return. No way would she step into that precinct again.

Her spine straightened. She wasn't done yet! Her best years were still ahead of her. She'd solve this mystery and get Dante back. That was her oath and she planned to keep it.

Riley dialed Rosita's number. Yes, it was late, but Rosita was a team player. Smart, intuitive, dedicated. A born leader that had gone overlooked and needed an opportunity to shine.

"Rosita! Thanks for picking up. I have a job for you."

"I'm listening."

"Dante was not kidnapped by Gino or the cousins, but someone else at the park that day. Someone who blended in so perfectly that no one would ever guess. A sociopath, who knew how to manipulate and walk behind a mask, unseen by their neighbors, their loved ones. You get it. A monster in sheep's clothing."

"That could be anyone, even people we know well. Want me to focus on locals or strangers?"

"For now, let's go over your list of volunteers. Anyone who might stand out, even though they knew how to blend in at the time. Tall order, I know. You can email it to me so I can get started once we land; I'll work through the night."

"I'll meet you there," Rosita said. "Two pair of eyes are better than one."

They both laughed and stopped abruptly.

"We will get this guy, Riley. And put him away for good."

Riley and Rosita didn't work alone. The whole team, C.C., Barnes, Matthew, and Stephan pulled an all-nighter in the breakroom, using the whiteboard to make a list of questions that required answers. Jeff and Elizabeth caught a few hours of shuteye then got the helo fueled up for a long day ahead. Monday. Twelve-thirty would tick the forty-eight-hour mark.

Using Rosita's spreadsheet and list of volunteers, one by one, they eliminated ninety percent of the people involved. Local volunteers, neighbors, and friends, were dismissed after a preliminary glance. Out of the hundreds of people at the Fourth of July celebration only a few outsiders had signed up as volunteers.

Riley studied the list of names with a fine-tooth comb. A couple of firemen who had come with their families for the day and lived in Bangor. Check. Several college kids had signed up, eager to do something. All good kids with no priors. Check. There were a couple of women who had been eager to help. One was assigned to Darren's team, the other who couldn't keep her mouth shut, bragging about her tracking experience, was in Rosita's group. They were both cleared but Rosita remembered how annoying the woman had become. High strung, wanting to claim her right to be a leader. Patricia Cabot. Riley put a question mark next to her name.

It was early dawn and Riley was beat, as was everyone in the breakroom. The passing of each moment was excruciating. Rosita straightened and asked, "Patricia Cabot. Why the question mark?"

"You thought she was obnoxious, pushing herself to the front of your group," Riley said. "I only saw her as an exuberant tourist with her Sandpiper Bay T-shirt and hat."

"She stayed until we came back to the park, but then she drifted away without a word and I never saw her again. I didn't mind since she'd been a nuisance with all her chattering." Rosita's eyes narrowed. "Let me try and call her."

Rosita dialed the contact number.

Riley made another pot of coffee.

"It's not an actual phone number," Rosita said.

Riley could have dropped an eyelash, and everybody would have heard it in that instant of total silence.

"Try again," C. C. said.

"Give me her address," Matthew said. "I'll do a reverse search."

Rosita copied it for him, and Matt raced to his office. Could this be the link they'd needed?

"Bingo!" Matthew cried as he returned. "No such name or address. We've been had."

"It's a common occurrence for the perpetrator to take part in the aftermath of the crime," C.C. said. "Usually with firebugs, but this too. The criminals think they are so much smarter than everyone else."

"She was telling us all about it wasn't she?" Riley asked, sick. "How she was an expert."

"We need to get a description of this woman out to the Coast Guard and the marina. Wyatt at the ferry," Barnes said.

Riley sank down to the chair. "This doesn't match the light-haired man theory."

C.C. clapped a hand on Riley's shoulder. "We are collecting information. Speaking of, Elizabeth is a decent sketch artist. Let's get her in here."

He called Elizabeth on the helo and ten minutes later both had entered the breakroom, Elizabeth with a tablet in hand.

"What did the woman look like?" Elizabeth asked Rosita first.

"She was my height, so five-foot-six give or take." Rosita leaned toward Elizabeth. "Cargo shorts with the pockets. A bright blue Sandpiper Bay T-shirt. Flip-flops. Leather."

"Hair color?" Rosita tipped her head. "Blonde. I think. It was short."

Matthew was humming with excitement. "I talked with the Tyler family last night and they'd reminded me that the woman with the light-haired angry man who was yelling was a blonde.

Also, that Shane remembered the name of the boat was Patty Girl."

"Patty? Short for Patricia? Cabot, not White. What's the connection? I feel like we're getting close. The boat has got to be gone by now." Her stomach roiled.

"Maybe not," Matthew said. "The bigger boat hit the dingy hard enough to destroy it. It had to have at least left a mark if not actual damage."

Elizabeth turned the tablet around with the image of fake Patricia. "That's her!" Riley said.

"It is. That's really cool," Matt said. "Can we get one of those for the station?" He looked at Barnes who shrugged.

"It's a pretty intuitive tool," Elizabeth said, "so you don't need to draw so much as remember details."

C.C. sat back at the desk. "If only we had confirmation of her name."

"Someday soon facial recognition will be a thing," Elizabeth said. "Patience, C.C."

"What now?" Barnes asked, stifling a yawn.

"Put Patricia Cabot into the system," Riley said. The hair on her arms rose.

Matt did the honors and five minutes later, he whooped. "Patricia Cabot—lives in Bar Harbor, and get this—her husband's name is Nathan Cabot."

"Barnes was right about Nathan using a fictitious last name," Riley said, giving credit where it was due.

"I'll send this out with a press of the button to our colleagues," Elizabeth said. "It's so early that our hands are tied." She glanced around the table. "I highly recommend a rest. Can we meet back here in an hour?"

At that news, a heavy weight fell over the group. Stephan stormed out, to do what was anyone's guess. To rip a few trees apart, Riley could only surmise.

"I'm fine," Matt said. "I have a great feeling that we will get Dante back today." He headed to his office.

Barnes didn't argue. "Rosita and Riley, go home. Let's meet back here in two hours."

"Deal," Riley said, stretching and yawning. "I want to see my family and assure them that I'm alive." She needed them to rejuvenate her sagging spirits. She hoped that Matt was right and today would be the day. As she left, she peeked in his office. Her partner was out like a light in his chair.

After a hearty breakfast and catching Kyra and her mom up to speed, she kissed them good-bye and headed down to the marina. It opened for business at eight and it was now half past. The expensive flashy boat that had run over the dingy played in her mind. It had to be Nathan Cabot. Where had he disappeared?

She was eager to speak with the owners of the marina, Bernie and Sally Murphy. Bernie supervised the boats and repairs while Sally managed the store that took care of the boaters' needs. She hadn't paid them a visit for weeks and it was more than due.

Bernie was helping a couple of men unload their 27-foot Boston Whaler. Looked like they'd had a lucky morning with two good-sized prized fish—one a striped bass, another a mako.

Riley waited until he was finished and then asked if he'd seen any large boats in for repairs over the weekend. Bernie took off his cap and scratched his head. His hair was a brilliant red. "Might have. Yep. July 4th, come to think of it. Fueled up and off they went. A couple. Seemed in a hurry too."

"No dents to speak of? I'm looking for something large that could have destroyed a dingy."

"An average boat could make mincemeat out of one if it were driven hard and made solid contact," Bernie said.

Great. "If you see it again, could you give me a call?"

"You've got it. Happy to oblige. Doesn't have anything to do with Dante, does it? He's a cute little kid. Trust me, I haven't seen him or any other kid on that boat you described."

"Thanks, Bernie. I'm going to poke around just the same."

"You do that, And good luck!" Bernie whistled a sailor's jig as she headed down the wharf.

What had she expected? A boat that matched, hiding in plain sight? Possibly named Patty Girl? Or Pretty Girl?

Riley knew she should get back to the station, but something held her back. She had a tingling feeling deep inside that had warned her before and she'd grown to trust it. She wished she had a copy of the blonde's picture. She texted Elizabeth asking her to forward the image to Riley's email.

Following her instinct, she entered the store and did a quick walkaround, then dawdled around the grocery section, picking up some fresh food. Salads and fruit, heathy snacks. On a whim she put a warm rotisserie chicken in her cart, then added another. There were hungry mouths to feed back at the precinct where she should be.

Riley stood a few feet behind a woman in a fashionable knit cap chatting with good-natured Sally and marveled at her patience. The lady had a lot to say about the small marina, the wait for maintenance, and lack of supplies. Her kid had a cold and there was no more cough syrup on the shelves. Riley stepped to the side and nodded at Sally, faking a yawn. Bernie's wife stifled a smile.

"Excuse me, won't you?" Sally apologized to the grumpy lady. "May I just take care of Officer Harper before we continue our chat?"

The woman huffed, annoyed, and turned to Riley with a hard gaze. Riley froze. It was her. Patricia the tracking lady.

Emotions careened through her body. Riley was armed. She needed to not alarm this woman so that she could contact Matthew and C.C. to swarm the marina.

Dante had to be here.

Hope warred with fear. Fear that she might be mistaken. She decided to play ignorant. "Oh, I don't mind waiting, Sally, but thank you. Your child is sick?"

"My daughter." She let out an elaborate sigh. "Completely under the weather and hasn't been sleeping or eating much for the past twenty-four hours."

The woman was a flat-out liar! "I'm so sorry to hear that." Riley's phone dinged with a notification from Elizabeth that she'd sent the email with the picture. She responded with a quick text back. *Come to the marina! Bring the troops!*

"Sleep is the magical cure for almost everything, right?"

"I'm sorry that we're sold out of the medication. Best thing would be for you to take her to a doctor. I could recommend one." Sally shuffled through her under-the-counter drawer, looking for a card.

"No! No doctor. We prefer the holistic approach to healing. Well, I won't keep you, Officer. Sally." She brushed past Riley, averting her face.

Riley abandoned her grocery cart and followed her. "Perhaps I can help. I have children of my own." She touched her arm. "Don't I know you from somewhere? Your face is familiar."

The woman yanked free from her light touch.

Riley had to stall for time and hope that Elizabeth understood the message. The marina was quiet on a Monday morning.

"Weren't you that nice lady who was an experienced tracker, helping us search for Dante Catalina?" At her deliberately neutral expression, Riley added, "You know, Fourth of July?"

"No, no, no. We weren't there." Her face turned a strange color of purple and Riley was worried she might conk out before they had Dante back with them.

"Here, let me help you sit down. You don't look so well."

The woman gave her a hex sign and ran away from Riley as fast as her bulky legs could carry her.

Riley followed slowly behind, texting every step of the way. "Barnes, Matt. I'm at the marina and have Patricia pinned. She's heading for the dock and the boat. She told Sally that she has a kid on board who isn't feeling well. Get here fast—I won't let her out of my sight."

CHAPTER SEVENTEEN

Patricia kept looking behind her, no longer running but moving away from the dock as quickly as she was able. In her rush, she stumbled over a rock and fell forward. Before Riley could approach her, she scrambled up and limped toward the water's edge at the end of the marina's property line. Only woods and small patches of grass were behind the large, unruly hedge which hid a narrow waterway leading out to sea.

Riley picked up her pace and was on her before she could round the bend and be out of sight. "Where do you think you're going?" She got so close that she murmured in her ear, "I know you don't have a daughter. Where have you stashed Dante?"

The frightened woman attempted to escape, slapping, and scratching but to no avail. Riley could hear the sirens becoming louder and the woman began to wail. "Why did you call him Dante?" she cried. "His name is Joseph, like in the bible. God's gift to me." Huge sobs ripped through her body, tearing her apart.

The sirens stopped as two SUVs and Matthew's sedan came to a halt, blocking them in so the woman couldn't get free. C.C.

grabbed her by the arms and handcuffed her. "It's over Patricia. He better be unharmed for both your sakes."

Barnes snapped. "Where is the boy?"

"You're too late. The boat...he's gone," Patricia threw her head back and laughed hysterically. "Like my other babies. Gone."

C.C. was already calling the Coast Guard who had the boat, Patty Girl, in their sights. Thanks to Matt's diligence with questioning the teens, they'd remembered the name of the boat and Matt had passed that information on.

"You better pray that he's well," Barnes hissed. "That's the only thing that might keep the two of you from a long prison sentence."

Swarmed by the two men in uniform, the woman dragged her feet as they pulled her toward the police car, opened the door, and not too gently shoved her in. Riley slid in next to the suspect, still breathing heavily from the ordeal.

"You can start talking now." Riley felt dirty sitting so close to her. "Let's start with your name, then your husband's name."

Patricia only glowered at her. "Nothin' to say. You'll never find him, ya know. Fish bait."

Riley's fist clenched and she gritted her teeth. "His mother is waiting for Dante's return. We have every reason to believe he's alive. The Coast Guard has already entered the boat and your husband is under arrest. Still want to remain silent?"

C.C. turned his head and winked.

Riley didn't know if her statement was true, but the wink lifted her spirits just the same. Having Barnes' and C.C.'s approval meant a lot. She had clawed her way back.

∼

The station was a mob scene. Rosita was there, Matthew, and Maria, Coby, Stephan, Elizabeth and Jeff. The helo waited outside.

Anticipation, excitement, and hope was a magical thing. The Coast Guard had Nathan Cabot under arrest and Dante was found, weak, fearful, but alive. They would arrive any minute. The FBI's stood at the door eagerly waiting to take their two prisoners back to stand trial.

In the past thirty minutes they learned all their secrets.

Patricia Cabot, Nathan Cabot's wife, had pretended to be an "experienced tracker" in order to be close to the planned kidnapping. She'd been able to steer them in the wrong direction with the misplaced sandal and had been the mastermind behind this terrifying ordeal. After three miscarriages she'd lost faith and was out of touch with reality.

Nathan's affair with Maria, where he'd posed as Nathan White, had lingered in Patty's mind and festered after each miscarriage. When she lost her last infant in June, Patty told Nathan that he owed her a child. He'd thought she would get over this fixation and had suggested they adopt, but she wanted revenge.

All Patty cared about was this Maria person who had her husband's baby, and she wanted that child whether it be a boy or girl. She believed he belonged to her, and nothing would stop her from taking this child.

Before the kidnapping she had approached Dante at the bubble machine and convinced him to come with her to meet his daddy who was waiting for him in Maccabee Park. Dante had been hesitant at first, knowing his mother would be angry if he left without telling her, but curiosity and Patty's insistence convinced him to go along—only for a few minutes as he knew his mom and Kyra would be anxious.

Once the plan was in motion, gentle-hearted Nathan suggested they go back to Dante's home to bring along some of his favorite things, explaining to the little boy that his mother had given her permission for Dante to spend the afternoon on the boat since she was busy working.

Patty sneaked away from the search party and joined Nathan and Dante at the designated spot where they had stashed the boat. The first hour went okay but as soon as Dante started to cry for his mommy, Nathan wanted to turn around. They began to argue until it turned physical, which is when Nathan lost control and hit the dingy. It didn't take long until he realized the hull of his boat was leaking. They could not go home as planned.

Hiding behind the marina, Nathan moored in a spot which was nearly impossible to see. He could not ask for help but went to the store and bought enough equipment to mend the large gaping hole in his boat, hoping it would hold for the ride home.

Each minute, each hour, and then days were fraught with danger. Patty would walk to the store and come back with water and enough food to last a day. Cold medicine to keep Dante quiet. They planned to sneak away in the early morning before the sun was up, but that night they had a brief storm which only lasted an hour but destroyed his patchwork. They were stuck again.

That was when Riley found Patty wanting to buy medicine that would keep Dante silent.

Dante's arrival was thrilling. Mother and son reunited again was both heart-breaking and wonderful. Not a dry eye was seen —excepting C.C. who remained stoic. Stephan swung the boy high as everyone stood and cheered.

Maria held her arms out for her son and Dante burst into tears. She settled him on her hip, brushing his dark curls from his pale forehead and exuding love as he snuggled in the protection of her arms.

Witnessing how the islanders had banded together had solidified Riley's choice to stay and be part of the story here.

Riley clinked her wine glass, which held a sweet pinot thanks to Rosita's thoughtfulness.

"Ladies and gentlemen." Riley smiled as everyone stopped chatting. "Our family has made an important decision. As you know, my contract was for one year and in five weeks it will expire, leaving us with plenty of options. I was on the fence for quite some time believing that this island might be too small and limiting. I want Kyra to expand her horizons and have adventures of her own. To become the best she can be and experience the world with no restrictions."

"What do you mean by small?" Matt teased. "To us, it's just the right size." His expression turned serious. "Don't tell me you're going back to Phoenix."

Riley let her gaze travel over Matt's dear face, Chief Barnes', who beamed with contentment, onto Dante cuddled in his mother's arms. Rosita. Coby and Maria. "No. We will remain in Sandpiper Bay for the next year—we think it's just right too. Kyra heads to Paris in a few days with other talented artists from her school, which is a terrific opportunity. Others will come, I know it. My mom loves it on the island, as do I. So, Chief Barnes, what will it be? One year, or two?"

Folks shuffled their feet as they looked from her to the chief and back again.

Barnes reached her in five steps and shook her hand. "You are welcome to be chief here in Sandpiper Bay as long as you want, and for Matthew to be your right-hand man. When you eventually leave Matthew will fill your shoes, and I know he's the man for the job. Right, Matthew?"

Matthew blushed and everyone cheered. He stood up and said a few words. During the applause, Riley slipped away. She had a date tonight—with her mom and daughter, and the lobster they'd been waiting for.

CHAPTER EIGHTEEN

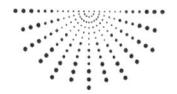

When Riley entered their rental house, she was warmly greeted with huge hugs and kisses and congratulations which brought tears of joy to her eyes. She patted them away, knowing she was in an emotional state of mind.

"We are so proud of you," her mother said.

Kyra patted her back. "You really are my hero."

"Enough!" Riley laughed. "Don't start me crying; or I might not stop."

Kyra and her mom were already dressed and ready to go.

"Okay then. I'm so hungry, Mom. I can taste the lobster already." Kyra gave her a gentle push.

Susan, in a summer dress, patted her stomach. "It tastes so good, doesn't it?"

Riley shook her head. "Okay, okay. I got the message." She took the stairs two at a time. Shedding her work clothes, she turned on the shower, allowing it to heat before stepping in. The warmth and feel of the powerhead pounding her flesh made her want to linger, but she didn't.

After a quick glance in her closet, she chose a flowing skirt and a white off-the-shoulder top. Feeling clean and feminine again, she applied a little makeup and smiled in the mirror. Not having enough time to wash her hair she tugged it into a knot that rested on the nape of her neck. A squirt of perfume and she was ready to go.

Moments later she entered the kitchen, and her family made a fuss over her once again. They all climbed into her SUV with plenty of room for each of them.

When they arrived at the Lobster Pot for their special dinner, Katie and her boyfriend Carter greeted the three ladies like royalty. This had been the first restaurant in Sandpiper Bay where they'd dined, and it wouldn't be their last. Carter grinned and like old friends he kissed both their cheeks, making Kyra blush.

"Great to see you all of you. Guess I better go shuck some oysters and prepare your lobsters just the way you like them." First time here, Riley and her family had never tasted lobster as they'd lived all their years in land-locked Phoenix. Carter, chef extraordinaire, had kindly offered to do the hard work, cracking the legs into large bites, and sliding out entire slices from the narrow claws.

Carter still enjoyed seeing the excitement on their faces and their delight as lemon butter dripped down their chins. They would normally come once a month on a Saturday night, and he never stopped spoiling them.

Katie cleaned up a table by the window as she too greeted them happily. "You get prettier every day, Kyra. All grown up and ready to leave the nest, I bet."

"Don't give her any ideas," Susan said with a twinkle in her eye. "She'll be off and running soon enough."

"Too soon." Riley gave her daughter a quick hug. "She'll be leaving on Sunday to go to Paris for ten days with school mates. It's for the students who are art majors and Riley was invited."

"Sounds wonderful," Katie said. "I was there as well many

years ago. I took culinary courses and stayed for two months. I was having too much fun to leave." She nodded toward the kitchen. "Carter was in Paris at the same time and convinced me to return with him. And here I am."

"Best place possible." Susan glanced over at Carter in the kitchen. "He's a gem."

"I know. I got lucky. Sometimes though I long to leave here and travel again like I used too." Katie sighed. "One day."

Susan was a wise woman. Riley watched as her mom leaned over and spoke quietly, "Be careful what you wish for and be happy with what you have."

Katie left to take care of new customers, and Carter arrived with a plate of freshly chucked oysters on a half shell, an even dozen. Like the lobsters he'd shown the ladies how to enjoy, he added a dab of horseradish, or cocktail sauce and a light squeeze of lemon. Then tossing the head back, they'd learned to slurp them down.

It had taken them a few months to acquire a taste, and enjoy the texture and taste, but once they did, they fell in love with the succulent treats.

Eventually the other diners in the restaurant petered out, and soon they were one of three tables left. The lobsters were excellent, and Riley hated to rush.

Carter had put the closed sign on the door and dimmed the lights as the last of the stragglers left. As a grand finale Katie and Carter brought over a key lime pie and sat down with them over coffee, pie, and conversation.

Riley was torn about revealing her recent announcement. She hadn't had a chance to tell Kyra and her mom but knew in her heart that this is what they both wanted. She acknowledged the fact that she wanted it too.

Taking a leap of faith, Riley clinked glasses with everyone at the table. "I have something important to say and yet I haven't had a chance to tell Mom and Kyra."

"It's okay, Mom. We already know."

"Know what?"

"That we're not moving. We are staying here for two more years." Kyra jumped from the seat and threw her arms around her neck. "I love you Mom, thank you!"

"Did you know too?" she asked her mom, seated opposite her.

"I knew that you'd make the right decision, and you did." Susan winked over her wine glass.

"But how…" Riley asked.

"Happy secrets are like butterflies in a setting such as this. Each one touches another, and another until the end of time." Her mom shrugged.

Kyra rolled her eyes. "Matthew called us when you were in the shower. I could tell from his excitement that something major had come up, so I begged him. Guess what? Your partner blurted it out right away."

Carter jumped up. "This calls for champagne. It's a wonderful day. Dante home safe, and our best friends are staying right here. Magnifico!"

Riley and her family nodded with tears in their eyes. They had found peace and love and acceptance on this tiny island and healed from memories of their past. The future looked bright again and Riley knew Sandpiper Bay would always linger in their hearts no matter how far and wide they drifted.

A forever home.

THE END

ABOUT AUTHOR TRACI HALL

From contemporary seaside romances to cozy mysteries, USA Today bestselling author Traci Hall writes stories that captivate her readers. As a hybrid author with over fifty published works, Ms. Hall has a favorite story for everyone.

Mystery lovers, be on the lookout for her Salem B&B Mystery series, co-written as Traci Wilton, and her Scottish Shire series, which takes place in the seaside town of Nairn, as Traci Hall.

Whether it's her ever popular By the Sea series, the next Appletree Cove sweet romance, or a fun who-done-it, Traci finds her inspiration in sunny South Florida, by living right near the ocean.

Writing as Traci Hall, Scottish Shire mysteries

Murder in a Scottish Shire July 2020
Murder in a Scottish Garden May 2021
Murder at a Scottish Social 2022

Traci Hall also writes historical romance, western romance, teen paranormal, new adult paranormal, coming of age, and non-fiction books.

Go to: TraciHall.com to learn more

ABOUT AUTHOR PATRICE WILTON

NEW YORK TIMES, bestselling author, PATRICE WILTON knew from the age of twelve that she wanted to write books that would take the reader to faraway places. She was born in Vancouver, Canada, and had a great need to see the world that she had read about.

Patrice became a flight attendant for seventeen years and traveled the world. At the age of forty she sat down to write her first book—in longhand! Her interests include tennis, pickleball, traveling, and writing stories for women of all ages.

She is best known as a popular romance author with 35 heartwarming stories on her resume. She is especially proud of her bestselling contemporary romance series, Paradise Cove, Heavenly Christmas, and the Wounded Warriors. Co-writing with Traci Hall, they have assumed the name Traci Wilton for the Salem B&B mystery series published by Kensington.

OTHER BOOKS BY TRACI HALL AND PATRICE WILTON

WRITTEN AS TRACI WILTON

Traci Wilton is a pseudonym of Traci Hall and Patrice Wilton. Patrice Wilton is the *New York Times* and *USA Today* bestselling author of more than thirty books, some indie-published and some published by Amazon/Montlake. Traci Hall is the USA Today bestselling hybrid author of more than 50 books from cozy mystery to romance. Visit them at traciwilton.com

Mrs. Morris and the Ghost August 2019

Mrs. Morris and the Witch 2020

Mrs. Morris and the Ghost of Christmas Past September 2020

Mrs. Morris and the Sorceress March 30 2021

Mrs. Morris and the Vampire August 2021

Mrs. Morris and the Pot of Gold 2022

A Note from the Authors:

Thank you for reading DANGER AT SANDPIPER BAY

If you enjoyed this book, I'd appreciate it if you'd help others

find it so they can enjoy it too.

- Lend it: This e-book is lending-enabled, so feel free to share it with your friends.
- Recommend it: Please help other readers find this book by recommending it to friends, readers' groups, and discussion boards.
- Review it: Let other potential readers know what you liked or didn't like about.

If you'd like to sign up for TRACI WILTON'S newsletter to receive new release information, please visit www.traciwilton.com

THANK YOU

Printed in the USA
CPSIA information can be obtained
at www.ICGtesting.com
LVHW041118300624
784337LV00020B/209